SOME DIE YOUNG

Dr Eric Fenton was made executor to the estate of a patient named Basil Porter. When the dead man's nephew, also named Basil Porter, mysteriously showed up, Dr Fenton found himself up to his neck in Arab [illegible], international intrigue and the Central Security Agency. Involved in [illegible] with strange medical complications and desperate because he felt sure they were [illegible] to be killed, Dr Fenton devised a plan to [illegible] his captors by helping them to [illegible] an aeroplane. He succeeded in [illegible], but [illegible] not he had [illegible] to halt the hijacker.

SOME DIE YOUNG

SOME DIE YOUNG

by

John Kilgore

Dales Large Print Books
Long Preston, North Yorkshire,
BD23 4ND, England.

British Library Cataloguing in Publication Data.

Kilgore, John
Some die young.

A catalogue record of this book is
available from the British Library

ISBN 1-84262-344-3 pbk

First published in Great Britain in 1970
by Robert Hale & Company

Published in Large Print 2004 by arrangement with
Robert Hale Ltd.

Dales Large Print is an imprint of Library Magna Books Ltd.

Printed and bound in Great Britain by
T.J. (International) Ltd., Cornwall, PL28 8RW

CONTENTS

CHAPTER ONE

THE UNHAPPY EXECUTOR

According to Eric Fenton, who was well qualified to make the judgement, Basil Potter had died in his sleep from a massive coronary occlusion. Furthermore, and also according to Dr Fenton, a man who had lived as Mr Potter had, over a period of seventy-seven years, had got only what was coming to him, and the marvel was that it had not occurred a quarter of a century earlier.

Basil Potter owned a publishing empire variously assessed by competitors and associates as being worth something in the neighbourhood of twenty million dollars. Also, he left behind a fabulous estate in the foothills north of San Francisco, as well as his empty seat as Board Chairman and Managing Director of his company, Potter Publications, Incorporated.

Eric Fenton had been Potter's physician for seven years, since Fenton had moved to the Golden State from the wall-to-wall confusion of New England, and although a good bit younger than his departed patient, had been the old man's friend.

They had not always got on very well. Eric Fenton, at fifty, was a fine physician, a wealthy man, a widower, and possessed of both a high opinion of himself and a sense of great integrity. Old Potter, on the other hand, had no education to speak of, had never been married, and said often, in print and out, that integrity was something only saints and rich hypocrites could afford.

He had clawed his way up, had a whole legion of enemies, and was frank in his dislike and distrust of other publishers, California land agents and Democrats.

After he had been tucked away in the exquisite marble crypt he'd had prepared years earlier, and which stood secluded in a grove of eucalyptus trees near the rear boundary-line of his Sierra foothill estate, the Potter Publishing Company solicitors produced an interesting surprise: Eric Fenton, denounced in the old man's Last Will and Testament as a holier-than-thou pill-pusher, had been nonetheless designated executor of the Basil Potter Estate.

That may have been why Dr Fenton said

Potter deserved that coronary occlusion a quarter of a century before he finally had it; the prospect of being executor for anything as complicated as the Potter Estate was quite enough to make a brave man blanch, or say something snide.

Furthermore, Eric Fenton had not come west to a limited and select practice, just to be victimized by a disagreeable old financial buccaneer to the extent that his telephone rang constantly, now, with people, purporting to be illegitimate offspring of old Potter, demanding a slice of all that wealth.

'I cannot and will not do this,' he told William Carnegie, of the New York City law firm of Carnegie, Duff and McGregor, old Potter's eastern-seaboard lawyers. 'If I must, I'll go to court and ask to be relieved. Even if I didn't have my practice, and even if I wanted a full-time occupation, I still wouldn't get involved in anything Basil Potter put together.'

William Carnegie was sympathetic. He was also gently obdurate. 'Doctor, by the time you could get a court out there to set that codicil aside and release you, the matter of the estate will have resolved into nothing more than a few hours daily of routine duties. For which Mr Potter made a very liberal salary available.'

Fenton was a large, grey, healthy, robust man. When he raised his voice, as he now did, no one ever afterwards complained of not hearing what he said. 'Mr Carnegie, I don't give a damn! I don't need that salary, and I will not be involved. If necessary I'll refuse to sign anything, to pass any judgements, to have anything at all to do with old Potter's confounded estate!'

'Doctor,' explained the suave lawyer, 'that wouldn't be a wise course to follow. In the first place, if you refuse, for example, to honour the funeral expenses, I have no doubt but that the funeral company will sue you. Not just the estate, but you personally. Then there is the matter of a dozen or so other bills pending; if they aren't paid – more lawsuits.'

Fenton turned red, but he only glared, he did not reiterate his obstinate position. Eventually he said, 'All right. But that's all I'll do. Authorize payment of the old devil's legitimate debts.'

Carnegie had his victory. 'If you wish, Doctor, we will hire a company of private investigators to find Basil Potter's heir. His brother's son. The man I'm sure Mr Potter must have told you disappeared several years ago in the Middle East.'

'By all means,' growled Fenton. 'Hire the investigator. Find that damned wastrel and get him back here.'

'Wastrel, Doctor?'

'That's what Basil called him. He even resented having the man named after him, although, as I told him at the time, it would be difficult to imagine anyone with old Basil's reputation having the gall to think anyone else named Basil could be one bit worse.'

Carnegie politely chuckled. 'May I ask what Mr Potter said to that?'

'He said I was a rotten doctor, a worse chess-player, and gulped down my sherry like a true peasant.'

Carnegie did not laugh this time although it was probable he would if he'd dared. Dr Fenton sighed and sat back and glared at the ceiling.

'He was a likeable rogue, in many ways, but he was one of the most unscrupulous men I've ever known, Mr Carnegie, and this is his idea of a big joke. He knew I did not approve of the way in which he had used people, even national governments, to create his empire and his fortune. He deliberately wrote that confounded will to have the last laugh.'

'Quite a laugh,' murmured William Carnegie. 'Doctor, we have been offered twenty million dollars cash, or a shares-transfer, for Potter Publishing, by one of the biggest newspaper syndicates in the world.'

'Well, take it.'

'Dr Fenton, is that your advice as executor?'

Fenton looked aghast. 'Do you mean to say that I am to pass judgement on this offer?'

'Yes, sir. As executor you have the obligation of–'

'That's enough,' roared Eric Fenton. 'Mr Carnegie, I will tell you again – I positively refuse to be that much of an executor. Find that damned nephew of Basil's and drop that thing into *his* lap.'

'Yes, sir, but I have a feeling finding Basil Potter the Third may be a long and drawn-out affair. Right at the moment American investigators aren't very popular in the Middle East.'

'Then hire an Arab,' said Fenton shortly. 'Or an Israeli, depending upon who happens to own the Middle East the day you send someone out. Just remember that I will not under any circumstances have anything to do with that damned estate, beyond paying whatever small bills the old devil left.'

That ended the discussions, and as far as Eric Fenton was concerned, the world could stand still to eternity before he would change his mind. He left William Carnegie with a feeling that this was definitely his last word on the subject. When Carnegie returned to New York and explained Dr Fenton's stand to his partners, they were not altogether surprised. In Carnegie's absence they had taken the liberty of having a very discreet run-down made on Eric Fenton. It had shown the physician to be an obstinate, humourless, tough-minded man of unimpeachable integrity, stuffy personality, considerable physical prowess in his younger days, the only child of a staunch pair of hard-shell Southern Baptists.

The only thing to do, of course, was locate the missing nephew. Of course, extreme precautions would have to be observed; heirs to the kind of wealth Basil Potter had left behind cropped up by the hundred, actually, every time a multi-millionaire died. There had recently been a case in the newspapers of a coloured man coming forth to swear up and down he was the son of an aged and very proper white woman of wealth who had died intestate. Even the medically proven fact that she had never had issue, had in fact been biologically incapable of ever having had offspring, did not deter the enterprising coloured man.

As for Dr Fenton, each time William Carnegie had occasion to telephone him from New York, usually over some debt that needed liquidating, he roared his frustrations all over again. Eventually, Carnegie adopted the wise course of waiting until he had quite a number of things to discuss before calling. In this way he was abused only once. The former method, of calling for each debt as it appeared, made Carnegie susceptible to a fresh outburst with each telephone call.

Finally, too, all the debts of record had been taken care of. Naturally, there was a deluge of fake ones inaugurated by merchants with the identical zealous cupidity of the coloured man, but it usually required only a little legal persuasion by Carnegie to have these quashed or withdrawn, usually when the merchant suddenly remembered that it hadn't been *Basil* Potter at all who owed them money, but someone named *Bill* Potter.

The company of high-priced investigators was also put to work. As Carnegie had occasion to tell Dr Fenton in order to ward off a virulent attack, these men were known in the East as the best in the nation at their vocation. They would undoubtedly locate the living Basil Potter – if indeed he were actually alive.

Three weeks after the old multi-millionaire had been buried, however, and despite something like a thousand dollars' worth of cables, the team of investigators began to sound pessimistic. At first Carnegie was inclined to believe this attitude might have resulted from the three Americans being incarcerated in Beirut, charged with being imperialist, warmongering, capitalist spies, but after this episode had been satisfactorily resolved through a liberal greasing of sandalwood-coloured palms, it developed that no one the investigators could find had ever heard of anyone named Basil Potter.

Fenton, in an outburst, said, 'Well, what in the hell did you expect? After all, that confounded name is known all over the world ... and not with any affection, my dear Carnegie. So your investigators must be utter fools to think they'll find this damned ninny just by going around asking for him by his proper name. What kind of investigators are these people you've hired? I might add, at great expense to the Potter estate!'

Better than most, Carnegie might have said, but he knew better by now than to cross Dr Fenton; all that ever produced was an even greater outburst. He trailed away by saying he would let Fenton know the moment anything turned up, and after ringing off, since it was by then five o'clock in New York, Carnegie closed his office and went downstairs to the little plush bar at street-level.

CHAPTER TWO

A MAN WITH A BROKEN LEG

The nearest village to the Potter estate was a drowsy, hill-hidden and tree-shaded place named Concord. Once, over a century earlier, during the Gold Rush, it had claimed a population of thirty thousand people, almost entirely male. Since those days, and despite the fact that from this area came ninety per cent of all the table wine produced in the United States, the population had dwindled to something like three or four thousand people, and had remained rather constant.

The village was a delightful place. Great trees shaded old homes and stores, mostly made of old-fashioned hand-made red brick. Main Street held all the commerce and there was no industry, not in Concord itself, but in the surrounding foothills wineries complete with stone vaults and acres of tended grape vines flourished.

Like all towns here the local well-being was dependent upon the minimal mechanization of a hand-industry, everyone was concerned with each crop-yield. In Concord people discussed the mild winters, the wet springs, and the magnificent coastal summers before they discussed politics. A drought, for example, made pithy, stunted grapes, which in turn, being largely unsaleable, depressed the local economy.

But also, after the passing of Concord's wealthiest neighbour, Basil Potter, speculation concerning the disposition of his vast wealth, for one whole summer at least, ran neck-and-neck with the traditional and customary concern for crop-yield.

Dr Fenton, whose semi-retirement did not

exclude him from caring for the local people because he could do it with a degree of paternalism that pleased him, was constantly being badgered by interested villagers.

Once when he showed exasperation over this innate curiosity, the man with the sprained back who had aggravated him with questions, and who owned the local hardware store – Chester Crittenden – succinctly put the local interest into proper perspective.

'Doctor, when a fortune like forty or fifty million dollars is involved, I don't care where or what you are, you're going to be fascinated. Around Concord no one in a whole lifetime makes as much money as Mr Potter's estate rakes in each year from the interest off one tenth of that fortune. People are entitled to be interested.'

Fenton's reply had been a grunt, then a disclaimer. 'In the first place, it's not a matter of fifty million dollars, Chester. An appraisal estimates the Potter fortune to be no more than thirty million, and perhaps even less.'

Crittenden rolled his eyes as though in supplication but he did not interrupt.

'In the second place, I think local interest is more earthy than interest or curiosity –

it's just plain nosiness. And finally, why keep asking me?'

'Because, Doctor, we get the *San Francisco Chronicle* up here just like they do down in the city, and it says you were appointed executor by the old man himself. So who should know if you don't?'

For Eric Fenton there did not seem to be any escape. When William Carnegie called from New York, from time to time, he did nothing to mitigate the physician's irritation. Not entirely because he only called when he needed Dr Fenton's judgement on some matter related to the estate, but also because he invariably had to report that while the prohibitive expense of the search for the lost heir continued, there were no encouraging results.

Only once did Carnegie escape Eric Fenton's vituperation. That was the day he called to say that a degree of success had been scored by the investigative team; they had got a trace of Basil Potter the Third. He had indeed been in the Middle East. As a matter of record he had studied Arabic in Damascus and the investigators had bribed his former teacher into revealing that Potter, using the name Bertram Porter, had been working on the translation of several ancient

Arabic manuscripts written in the years between A.D. 1100 and 1170, and giving first-hand, eye-witness accounts of the Crusades.

Dr Fenton had trouble in squaring that with what old Potter had told him of his wastrel nephew. 'Are you sure it's the right man?' he asked Carnegie. 'Mr Potter led me to believe his nephew was a large, easy-going, wenching, hard-drinking young man, and you'll have to admit this doesn't sound like a person who would learn a difficult language just so that he could read some musty old books.'

Carnegie was positive. 'Those were exactly our sentiments, Doctor, so we bought several papers from the old scoundrel who taught him Arabic in Damascus, had them brought over, and – verified Basil Potter's fingerprints from them.'

Fenton liked that. 'Very good, Mr Carnegie. It's the first flash of brilliance you people have shown thus far. And where is Mr Potter now?'

'He went to Paris, then to London. Still using the name Bertram Porter.'

'Yes. Well, spare me the details; just tell me where he is now.'

'We don't know, Doctor.'

Fenton's ire rose up. 'Do you mean to say that in a city as cosmopolitan as London your investigators can't find him?'

Carnegie tried appeasement. 'Doctor, they are still searching, and I think it's reasonable to assume that if they picked up the trail in a place like Damascus, they surely will find it again in London.'

'At a thousand dollars a day,' exclaimed Fenton pithily, 'they had better find it, Mr Carnegie, and soon. Or could it be that they have become accustomed to this fee and hope to prolong the search?'

Carnegie was either shocked at this suggestion of impropriety, or feigned shock, because he said, 'Doctor, these people have an excellent reputation for integrity.'

'Maybe,' growled Fenton. 'But not for results. Well, keep me posted.'

Carnegie agreed and rang off. Dr Fenton, who lived in a lovely cottage on a hilltop overlooking miles of rolling vineyards, stoked a pipe and went out upon his favourite verandah in the golden sunshine to ponder the conflicting reports of Basil Potter's character.

Old Potter had possessed the kind of vindictive nature that could colour anyone he disliked in the most unflattering shades. It was entirely possible, then, that Carnegie's report of this different heir and namesake was closer to being correct.

Probably, though, Fenton thought, the real Basil Potter the Third was an amalgam; a composite of both Carnegie's scholar and old Potter's vagabond wastrel.

Fenton concluded that the missing nephew must be an interesting man, whatever his character and personality. Non-conformists, if they had worthwhile intelligence, usually were. The trouble was, of course, that non-conformity was the popular vogue among the unwashed and infantile, or, as Eric Fenton had once called them, 'the mentally wounded'.

He was roused from his pleasant reverie by Mrs Smith, his widowed housekeeper, a husky woman in her no-nonsense forties. A grape-farmer by the name of Peter Silvera had rung up to ask if the doctor could visit his place at once and look at a labourer who appeared to have broken a leg in a tumble from a packing-shed platform.

Fenton could go, and since it was an emergency he most certainly would do so, but as he told Mrs Smith, no man *appears* to have a broken leg. 'He either has one or he has not, and you don't have to be a physician to know which it is.'

Mrs Smith never disputed things beyond the range of her household duties, but this time she had an observation to make that was quite true. 'Pete Silvera is a very polite man, Doctor. I knew his parents when I was a child. They came to America from Portugal in 1911. The old-time Portuguese were very polite and considerate, and most of them settled in Northern California, as you certainly must know by this time. Pete knows a broken leg when he sees one. He's just too polite to act like he knows your business.'

Properly put in his place, Dr Fenton drove serenely to the Silvera farm, a hundred and sixty acres of rich, scenic, rolling land, given over almost entirely to grapes. The house was low and very old and thriftily white-washed, and clean. There was shade all around it. Even the packing-shed and the little migrant-labour shacks were clean and shaded.

The impression one got upon leaving one's car in the cool broad yard in front of the Silvera residence was of thrift, self-respect, and a modicum of hard-wrung prosperity. Silvera himself was a dark-eyed, blackheaded man with a wonderful smile, thick body, and a shy sloe-eyed little wife who flashed a smile to Dr Fenton then was not seen again as her husband took the medical man round to the back of a vine-shaded old flagged patio where a large, powerfully-built youngish man with bold blue eyes and a reddish three-day beard, lay flat out upon a trestle-table.

Pete Silvera felt a need to explain as though this unusual resting place for the injured man reflected upon his hospitality.

'He insisted, Doctor. My wife and I wanted to put him to bed in the house until you came. He said the table was best.'

Fenton studied the man's hard, steady eyes, his square-jawed rather handsome Saxon face, and nodded. 'The gentleman was right, Mr Silvera. A hard table in most cases of this nature is preferable to a soft bed. Well now, suppose you tell me how it happened while I get to work, eh?'

Silvera shrugged and looked at the patient. 'These things happen, Doctor. Crushed grapes underfoot are as bad as grease. He simply slipped off the platform as he was leaning to put several crates upon a truck-bed.'

Fenton had the man's trouser-leg slit and put aside. He paused to glance at his patient, his expression wry. Dr Fenton had never encountered any difficulty in being sarcastic, as now, when he said, 'Do you speak English?'

The worldly blue eyes rested upon Fenton for a moment, mockingly, then the injured man answered. 'And Arabic, Dr Fenton.'

It wasn't the answer that shocked Eric Fenton, although it most certainly helped, and it wasn't the man's appearance, although it most certainly fitted the descriptions he'd had of Basil Potter the Third; it was some kind of abrupt and certain rapport that hit him like a physical blow with the knowledge that this was the man William Carnegie's investigators were rummaging London for.

He came upright and stepped back for a closer look at his patient. 'What is your name?' he asked quietly.

The tough, mocking eyes did not waver as the man replied. 'How about Joe Smith, Doctor? Are you going to splint the leg or shall I walk down to town and hunt up the veterinarian?'

Fenton was a large, confident, tough man himself, but the stranger was his match. He felt it even as he said, 'You couldn't walk fifty feet, Mr – Smith.'

'No? Care to wager on it?'

Fenton looked helplessly at Peter Silvera, who felt the antagonism on his shaded patio and was completely mystified by it. The injured man had come to work for him only four days earlier; Pete was certain his employee had never met Eric Fenton before. But there they were acting like old enemies. Pete could only shrug in response to Fenton's look.

The patient pointed. 'The leg, Doctor, the leg. I realize there is plenty of time before a swelling makes splinting difficult, but lying on this damned table isn't something I've always looked forward to.'

Fenton returned to work. For ten minutes his large, very capable hands did what had to be done. Once, when he went to fetch something from his car and Silvera was alone with his employee, the injured man smiled and said, 'Pompous medical men – and most are – disgust me.'

Silvera's black brows shot straight up. 'But you don't even know him, and he's a very good doctor. You embarrass me acting like that, Joe. It doesn't hurt to be courteous, does it?'

Joe kept smiling. 'Pete, would you like to make a friend for life? A glass of red wine, please.'

Silvera departed to get the wine, Dr Fenton returned, and Joe Smith lay there gazing at Fenton without a speck of amiability in his face for the man who was helping him.

Before Silvera returned, but when he was putting the finishing touches upon his handiwork, Eric Fenton said, 'This is only temporary. When you come over to my place I'll put a proper cast on it. Actually, it's not too bad a break. But I'll verify that, too, when you drop by, with an X-ray.' Fenton turned and looked into the younger man's beard-stubbled face. 'Your name is not Joe Smith. It isn't even Bertram Porter. Will you please explain to me what this charade is all about, Mr Basil Potter?'

The tough-eyed man said, 'You forgot, Doctor – the Third.'

Fenton nodded. 'So I did. Please excuse me. Well...?'

'Are you finished with the splint, Doctor?'

'Yes. For the time being. Until you can get over to my office, where I live.'

The younger man eased himself into a sitting position. 'I'm not coming over to your office,' he said.

CHAPTER THREE

VERBAL SKIRMISHING

Dr Fenton rarely argued with people. He had not the temperament for it; he became irascible too quickly, as William Carnegie could attest. But neither did he readily concede to any opposition in order to avoid argument, although in the case of the man with the broken leg he knew, just from standing there on Pete Silvera's patio exchanging looks with Joe Smith, neither a stubborn insistence nor a fierce argument would prevail.

So he tried patience, even though it definitely was not his paramount virtue. 'Look; if you'd prefer we won't mention your name or antecedents. But that damned cast is simply an improvisation. What's the sense of risking a limp for the rest of your life just to avoid visiting my cottage?'

The man with the reddish-auburn beard-stubble smiled with candid insolence. 'I simply prefer another doctor.'

'Should I ask why? Have I done something here that has made you question my ability? I could tell you, Mr Smith, that I have honours from–'

'Spare me,' said the younger man, still insolently smiling. 'You did a bang-up job with the splint and I'm sure you have an office full of framed attributes.'

Silvera returned, bearing two glasses, not just one, full of red wine. He brought none for himself; drinking wine when one was working hard produced too much perspiration. He handed Fenton a glass, then frowned slightly as he passed Joe Smith the other glass. He had evidently overheard part of the continuing skirmish between those two while inside the house. Then he smiled and pointed to the ruby-clearness of the red wine.

'We put that down in 1962, a perfect year. Not too much fog, not too little rain.' He waited expectantly for them to taste. When they did he smiled afresh. 'Well?'

'Sweeter than the best of France,' said Joe Smith. 'Softer than Mateus from Portugal, Pete.'

Dr Fenton drank his wine as if it was medicine or tepid water; in haste. Still, he tried to be gallant because he knew how the natives felt about their wines. 'Very good, Mr Silvera.' He put the half-emptied glass aside. 'Frankly, it makes me drowsy when I drink at midday, and because I still have to drive back...' He gave a small apologetic smile that entreated understanding. The plain fact was that Eric Fenton did not care for wine, not even very good wine. Old Basil Potter had been right when he'd accused Dr Fenton of drinking wine like a peasant.

There was a moment of awkwardness as the three men lingered in silence. Then Fenton complained to Pete that his employee did not intend to seek further treatment for his leg. Silvera's dark, baffled look drifted to the man sitting upon the trestle-table. 'Joe, do like the doctor says. Look; my workmen's compensation insurance takes care of everything. It won't cost you a dime, and if you're thinking of me, it won't increase my premium; I'm entitled to six accidents like this one every picking and packing season. So go, will you?'

Smith finished his wine, put the glass down and shook his head. 'Can't do it, Pete. And since I'm useless to you now, I'll catch a ride to town and be on my way.'

Silvera was almost insulted. 'On your way? Joe, you broke that damned leg on my ranch, doing work for me. You can't leave. We'll fix up a separate shack for you.'

Smith laughed and reached out a powerful hand to slap Silvera affectionately. 'I'll tell you something, Pete: I've spent ten years wandering all over this lousy world, and everywhere I've been, without exception, the only people I could ever identify with were the ones like you.'

Silvera had to think this over. So did Dr Fenton, but at least with him a quick conclusion could be drawn. He said, 'Mr Smith; is that it – you're some kind of earthy humanist? You have a different philosophy from most of us?'

Smith shrugged. 'Maybe that's it, Doctor.'

Fenton said, 'All right. More power to you. As I said before – not a word of recrimination, not a bit of probing. Just let me properly cast that leg, then you can certainly be on your way.'

Smith's tough glance narrowed in sceptical assessment. Silvera hung there waiting for the answer, his head almost imperceptibly bobbing up and down. Smith took his cue from that and nodded. 'Let's go, Doctor.' He eased down off the table. When Fenton reached forth to offer a hand Smith brushed it aside and leaned upon his employer.

Fenton flushed, turned and led the way out to his car.

He was a lot less annoyed with Smith than he was with himself; he had promised to do nothing that would compel Smith to admit his true identity, yet if Smith did *not* reveal it, Dr Fenton was going to have to continue in his hated role as executor of that damned old devil's ill-begotten estate.

Fenton was silent through the flowery goodbyes between Silvera and Joe Smith. He was also silent on the delightful drive back through the rolling countryside towards his hilltop cottage. Smith seemed to accept his silence as though it were the most natural thing in the world. He had not impressed Eric Fenton as a particularly loquacious man under any circumstances.

When they reached the cottage Mrs Smith came out to lend a hand. She was by nature a sympathetic, tolerant person. When Dr Fenton mentioned the injured man's name, she looked quickly up into his face, then shook her head. 'Not from around here, Doctor. I know 'em all and am related to 'em all.'

Joe Smith laughed at her, it was a rolling, infectious sound so she smiled back. 'Not that I'd mind,' she said.

Fenton's small office consisted of two rooms, one a combination office-examination room, the other a bit larger but still not very expansive room, equipped with the latest and best equipment he might need as a general practitioner. He put his patient upon the stainless-steel tiltable table in his second room, dismissed his housekeeper and went to wash his hands at the sink in a corner. With his back to Smith he said, 'Will you please answer one question for me – why?'

Smith rolled his head to look at Fenton's back. 'I thought we agreed – no probing.'

Fenton turned, towel in hand. 'We did. But there is something I think you should know. Your confounded uncle made me his executor, and I want to get out from that.'

'It undoubtedly pays well, Doctor,' said Smith, rolling his head back and staring at the ceiling.

'Mr Potter, I don't need the money and I damned well don't want it.'

'You must be an unusual doctor,' murmured Smith, still looking upwards.

Fenton flung aside the towel and walked forward. Smith was very hard on his disposition, which was always yeasty even at its best. 'I don't want to argue with you, Mr Potter. All I want you to do is contact your uncle's legal firm in New York City, Carnegie, Duff and McGregor – talk to William Carnegie – and for heaven's sake face up to the responsibility of your inheritance, man. How many people on earth would give anything to be in your position? Millions upon millions of them. All right; be a non-conformist if you choose, but please don't do it at my expense.'

Smith, or Basil Potter the Third, finally lowered his hard blue eyes. 'Fix the damned leg,' he growled, and gave Eric Fenton stare for stare. 'Shut up, Doctor, and fix the damned leg!'

Eric Fenton snapped erect, colour suffusing his face. Even as a young man, before achieving wealth and position and independence, people had not very often dared to use either that tone of voice or that kind of language to him. He stood with clenched fists battling with himself.

Smith calmly turned his head, saw the wrath in the older man's face and quietly said, 'Doctor, if you deserve any explanation from me it's only because of something perhaps neither of us could avoid – an old pirate's death. So I'll tell you this much. The minute I claim an inheritance, or do anything at all that will put my picture in the newspapers, I'll be able to count off the days on one hand – two at the very most – before I'm killed.'

Fenton, a lifelong and thoroughly domesticated member of the law-and-order Establishment, loosened his fists, let his anger fade, and eventually considered his prone companion with a troubled, even mystified, expression. He had never expected Basil Potter to turn up as any example of rare and exalted virtue, but what this man had just said implied a lot more than just wenching and drinking.

'If you would clarify that,' Fenton said, 'it would help me understand.'

Smith shook his head a little wearily. 'I'm not going to clarify it. And you don't have to understand. Now can we get on with the leg?'

The tough, stubborn blue gaze left Fenton no alternative. He went to work, but without haste because he had some thinking to do. The utter silence of his office, of his household on its low and secluded hilltop, made it possible for him to concentrate. As for preparing the leg-cast, he could have done that with both eyes closed.

Eventually he said, 'If you have broken a law I'm sure Carnegie, Duff and McGregor can protect you. If you haven't broken a law, Mr Potter, I'm equally certain you can either rely upon local police, or hire a squad of armed guards if you prefer – you'd certainly be able to afford it – to look out for you. But in any case I think you should know that I fully intend to see that your uncle's lawyers are told that you were here. Not because I want to put you in any peril, but because I simply don't want to have to go on being the executor of that damned Potter estate.'

Smith smiled. 'Doctor, you are jumping to a conclusion.'

'Am I? About what?'

'I have not told you that I am Basil Potter.'

Dr Fenton worked for a moment in dour silence, then looked up. 'And I haven't told you, Joe Smith, that I have your fingerprints all over this confounded office, and in my car, and I propose to have them checked to prove that you *are* Basil Potter!'

Smith's eyes twinkled through his tough smile. 'For an overgrown stuffed-shirt, Doctor, you're no simpleton. How is the cast coming?'

'It's coming very well. If you had both your legs I think I'd knock you down, Mr Potter.'

That brought a harsh laugh. 'Doctor, if I had both my legs – and one hand tied behind me – you couldn't do that. By the way, you don't happen to smoke, do you?'

'Yes. A pipe occasionally.'

'Then you'd have no cigarettes,' said Smith-Potter and fell to studying the ceiling again. 'It doesn't matter. Not good for me anyway, are they?'

Fenton had a rare stroke of macabre humour. 'Why not? If you aren't going to live more than a couple more weeks, why worry about heart disease or cancer?'

That brought forth another deep, infectious laugh from the man with the injured leg. His eyes dropped to Fenton's heavy profile. 'Tell me something, Doctor. How did you ever manage to be appointed executor of that old scoundrel's estate? I can't imagine two more incompatible people.'

'We were incompatible, yes,' answered Fenton, speaking slowly and thoughtfully. 'But in some ways your uncle was a fascinating personality. He was unscrupulous, but he was also oddly compassionate. He was suspicious and vindictive, but with a wonderful grasp of life in all its meanings. We argued rather fiercely at times, but I suppose you could say we were friends – in a peculiar way – and as for being executor, your uncle was an inveterate practical joker. He probably laughed himself to sleep every night after he had me written into his will as his executor, knowing how I would detest it.' Fenton looked up, straight-faced. 'Are you answered?'

'Better than you think,' said Smith, and did not offer to elaborate.

The cast was finished. Actually, it was a pre-cast implement, made in two separate parts, that was adjustable and resolutely reliable, another innovation in the field of therapeutics that minimized the error factor and saved time for the person who had to apply it.

When Fenton allowed his patient to sit up, the leg supported across the back of a chair, he said, 'Mr Potter, you aren't going very far wearing that thing. If you'll take my advice you'll let me keep you here at least until you can get by with nothing more cumbersome than a leg-brace.'

The younger man shook his head. 'I'll manage.'

Fenton had an ace-in-the-hole. 'Perhaps you will, Mr Potter, but so will I – and so will the private investigators who will be looking for you; you can't cover very much ground incognito wearing a leg-cast, can you?'

CHAPTER FOUR

DOCTORS ARE FALLIBLE – OR ARE THEY?

No amount of persuasion, or even mild threats, would induce the man with the broken leg to stay at the cottage.

In the end Dr Fenton agreed to drive him down to the village where he could buy a ticket on the daily coach that passed through, and, as before when they were driving along together, neither had anything to say.

Fenton shook his head. Granting that the injury was not really all that serious, it was still the height of something or other for Potter to insist on leaving. Even, as Fenton said at the bus depot, if the injured man only remained around Concord for three or four days, it would minimize his chances of bumping or otherwise aggravating the condition of the leg.

Smith-Potter thanked Fenton for all he'd done, wearing his same hard and uncompromising smile throughout, then hobbled off to buy his bus ticket. Fenton went at once to the branch office of the telephone company, put in a long-distance call for William Carnegie, and was thoroughly frustrated when he was coolly informed by Mr Carnegie's secretary in New York that the lawyer would not be back in his office until the following morning.

Fenton went out and sat in his car wondering whether he dared go to hunt up the local constable and try to get him involved. Common sense told him, since Smith-Potter had done nothing illegal, at least as far as Fenton knew, the constable would simply refuse to intervene.

He was still sitting in the car when the bus arrived in the village, took on its solitary new passenger and departed northward, in the general direction of Nevada, which lay northward through the Sierra passes.

Finally, admitting defeat, Fenton drove home, had lunch in a surly mood, went to clean up his little clinic, and later put in another call for William Carnegie, this time insisting that the cool-toned secretary contact her employer at once and tell him to return Fenton's call.

He must have sounded convincing; Carnegie rang him up in less than an hour.

Fenton told him the entire improbable story and Carnegie was flabbergasted. He kept questioning Fenton about the stranger's identity, his strongest reason being the last report from the investigators in London.

'It's so *unlikely*,' he said. 'Why would the man be out there, and if that was him, why would he refuse to identify himself, or claim the inheritance?'

'My dear Mr Carnegie,' said Fenton with considerable forbearance, 'I haven't the faintest damned idea why he acted that way. The only clue was the remark about being in physical peril if his picture appeared in the newspapers. I think we'll have to agree that in a case of inheriting vast wealth, or staying alive, most men would prefer staying alive.'

'But what could he be involved in?'

'*I* don't know,' exclaimed Fenton.

'And you're really satisfied it was Basil the Third?'

'Yes. If you'll send one of those eminent investigators of yours out here I'll show him at least a dozen fingerprints. We can then verify the man's identity.'

'First thing in the morning. And assuming that this really was our man, where will we find him now? It's too bad you couldn't have detained him in some way.

'My God,' roared Fenton, 'isn't a broken leg enough to slow down most people? Carnegie, I talked myself blue in the face. He is a very difficult person. I'll even go farther and say that he struck me as a man who could become very disagreeable, if he chose to be. I tried everything and none of it worked. I considered calling in the police, even.'

'If you had,' replied Carnegie, 'and it wasn't Basil Potter, you could have ended up being sued for false arrest.'

'Carnegie,' said Fenton, lowering his voice under considerable effort, 'I tell you it *was!*'

'Yes, Doctor. I'll see to it that a man from that investigative agency gets right out there to look at those fingerprints. Meanwhile, may I suggest that you find out, if you can, where this man was going; the people at the bus depot should remember his destination.'

Fenton agreed to look into that, and he did it that same afternoon, barely reaching the depot before five-o'clock-closing-time.

There was no difficulty in identifying the stranger; apart from his leg being in an obvious cast, he had been the only person to depart from Concord that day. His destination had been listed as Reno, Nevada. He had bought a ticket for cash that far north.

Fenton drove back to his cottage slowly and thoughtfully. Smith-Potter's revealing remark about being in danger settled into the forefront of Fenton's awareness. Maybe what he should do was be very careful, not just because he certainly had no wish to jeopardize Smith-Potter's safety, but also because if anything should happen to the confounded man, Fenton would then have to stay on as executor of the estate.

He made himself a stiff whisky-and-soda before dinner, took it out to his favourite vantage point on the patio, and drank it slowly in a troubled and irritable mood.

He had worked hard to achieve his semi-retirement. His life since coming to this isolated area of California had been pleasant, comfortable, altogether satisfactory. And now, because he had cared for an ailing old scoundrel, he was involved in something that certainly had overtones of violence. He finished the drink. Even if he'd remained in the East, where physical danger was always near at hand, he probably wouldn't have ever found himself in any worse situation.

Mrs Smith came to tell him his dinner was ready. He grunted and went back into the house. The sun was nearly gone, an immense red globe that each day dropped behind some saw-toothed distant rims, but it still managed to be nearly eight o'clock. Of course, it being summertime made that possible.

Otherwise, Dr Fenton's world was orderly, systematic, comfortably predictable, and a man with a broken leg who had declined to clutter it up with whatever he was involved in should perhaps have been thanked for that. Instead, Eric Fenton ate his dinner without tasting a bit of it, and afterwards decided to drive over to the Silvera farm to see what he could glean from a man who had known the stranger four days.

It was a dry run. Dr Fenton probably should have known it would be, if he'd paused to make an evaluation; Smith-Potter, assuming he really was in peril, would hardly take into his confidence someone he had only just met.

Silvera showed Fenton the labourer's shack where Smith-Potter had stayed, showed him the man's signature on several papers having to do with his employment, and finally asked the inevitable question.

'What's it all about, Doctor? Did he steal a car or something?'

Fenton could answer only providing he was prepared for the turmoil his suspicions concerning the stranger's identity were certain to produce throughout the entire countryside. He was not willing to go through that, so he simply said the man's behaviour had been so unique he couldn't help but be interested.

Silvera, a simple man, was satisfied. He also concurred. 'Before you came he was as friendly as anyone who has ever worked here, Doctor. But the moment he saw you, he changed. Maybe, as my wife said, he had something against doctors. Or maybe it upset him because he broke his leg at the peak of the season; you know how it is with these migrant people; they can only make a good living for a few months out of the year.'

Dr Fenton agreed that perhaps it was any one of these things, of maybe even all of them together, and got back to his car for the drive home knowing nothing more than he had known before.

He had to be content with this, but he

made himself another highball before going off to bed, and that indicated his state of mind because he had never been, and was not now, much of a drinker – and least of all a *wine* drinker.

The following morning the special investigator Carnegie had sent arrived before noon in a rented car. He was a brisk, pleasant, cold-eyed and thin-lipped man who declined Dr Fenton's offer of lunch on the grounds that he had eaten after leaving San Francisco for the northward drive, and would like to get right to work. Dr Fenton was very obliging; he showed him Smith-Potter's fingerprints in the clinic and in his private car out in front, then Dr Fenton watched, interested because he had only seen the procedure on television before, while the special investigator dusted each latent print, brushed the best ones up to their maximum visibility, photographed them with a magnifying lens, and after somewhat over an hour of this delicate work, put all his equipment together and with little more than a nod to Dr Fenton, departed as quietly and swiftly as he had arrived.

It was all very entertaining. It was also impressive. The investigator had quite obviously been well trained and experienced at his work. Perhaps Carnegie had been correct after all, about the reputation of that man's agency.

Not until evening did the impatience begin to wear at Dr Fenton's nerves. He consulted his watch, estimated the length of time it should have taken for that investigator to reach New York City, added another couple of hours for the fingerprints to be compared with Basil Potter's known prints, and sighed because even if the man had made all his connections right on schedule there probably could not be anything revealing for several more hours.

He went to bed that second evening after the departure of the man with the broken leg feeling more frustrated than ever. Wherever the man with the leg-cast now was – Reno very probably – Fenton was justified in feeling concerned over the probability that the man was slipping away from him.

He had, however, under-estimated that prestigious New York private investigative agency.

The following morning shortly after breakfast, and allowing for the time-differential between San Francisco and New York City, Dr Fenton telephoned William Carnegie. He was obliged to ring back an hour later because Mr Carnegie had not arrived at his office yet.

He rang back but in very poor grace. When Carnegie finally came to the telephone Dr Fenton said, 'Well, now are you satisfied that my man was Basil Potter the Third?'

Carnegie cleared his throat, made a sort of gentle but audible sigh, and said, 'Doctor, believe me, I most sincerely hate to tell you this, but–'

'*What!*' exploded Eric Fenton. 'But that's not possible, Carnegie!'

'Doctor, please calm down. And I'm afraid that it most certainly *is* possible. The man who left his fingerprints in your car and your operating-room, or whatever it is, bears the name Floyd Merritt. For your further information, Doctor, Floyd Merritt is an ex-convict from Joliet Penitentiary in Illinois with a police record for felonies half as long as your arm.'

Dr Fenton groped for the chair beside his desk and sank down upon it. 'Carnegie,' he said in a very earnest tone of voice, 'how could some criminal named Floyd Merritt know who I was? Don't interrupt, please; that man definitely knew who I was when he first saw me at the Silvera place. I can't explain *how* he knew, but take my word for it, he knew me. How could he know that, and how could he have known about old Basil Potter?'

'The newspapers perhaps...?' murmured Carnegie in a fading voice.

'No! I tell you, Carnegie, there is something terribly wrong here.'

The lawyer did not argue this point. He simply said, 'Doctor, for your information we sent *two* investigators to California yesterday. One came to see you, the other one is still tracing your gentleman with the broken leg. When he finds him and verifies his identity through the police, I'll call back and let you know. Now, much as I don't like to have to leave you, Doctor, I've got to keep an appointment...'

Fenton put aside the telephone, fished for his pipe, stoked it with great care, lit up and leaned back to smoke – and think.

Somewhere, there was a very definite and glaring inaccuracy and he was as positive as he could be that it was not *his* inaccuracy.

Of course, Carnegie, not having been there to see that stranger, and hear him, could not be blamed for his scepticism. But Carnegie was damned wrong and sooner or later it was going to be evident that this was so!

CHAPTER FIVE

A WRECKED LADY

Dr Fenton had an emergency appendectomy the next morning at seven o'clock. It proved to be a near thing and he was not prepared to handle major surgery. His customary procedure was to refer the seriously ill to city hospitals.

In his favour, appendectomies were old hat. In the East he had performed hundreds, all successful. This one, performed in great haste at a farm, was also successful, but when he finally got away from there a little while before noon, he felt wrung out.

He drove back to Concord, was accosted by the constable, a burly, pleasant man named George Elah, and taken to the local dentist's office just off Main Street where a voluptuously lovely young woman was resting on a sofa in the dentist's private office, badly shaken as the result of losing control of her car on a curve east of town, and having struck a large tree. The car, according to Constable Elah, had a bashed-in front end but otherwise was not damaged.

Fenton asked the girl her name and where she felt pain. She had a headache, she told him, and was a little sick to her stomach, and her name was Irene Buford. She had been passing through, northward, on her way inland from San Francisco.

Fenton suggested moving her to the hotel, after he had made his examination without finding any sign of serious or even moderate injury, and in fact supervised this transition, making sure she was comfortably resting before going to a nearby café for a cup of coffee. There, he encountered the burly, amiable constable, who was eating a horse-sized luncheon.

'Sure pretty,' said the constable. 'Damned lucky she wasn't going any faster when her car left the curve and hit that tree. Even luckier, I'd say, that I was on my way back to town after delivering papers on a foreclosure in the foothills.'

Fenton lifted his coffee cup, saw the tip of a wallet-size photograph peeping from Constable Elah's shirt pocket and said, 'Where did you get that picture, Constable?'

Elah paused in his eating to give Fenton a blank look. 'Picture? Oh! Oh, you mean this thing?' He pulled the photograph from his pocket and tossed it down. 'I meant to give it back to her and plumb forgot. It must have fell out of her purse at the impact. It was on the seat of her car.'

Dr Fenton lifted the little photograph, studied the tough blue eyes, the rust-auburn hair and the hard smile. There was nothing written on the back of the picture, and it looked as though the photograph might have been taken some time back, perhaps a year or two, because the face was fuller, less stressed and lean and shadowed, but there was no mistaking the identity of the man with the broken leg.

Dr Fenton sighed, put the photograph down and finished his coffee. He sat for a while longer with Constable Elah, then departed.

Outside, Main Street looked as drowsy in summer shade as it always looked. The temperature was pleasantly cool. A dog lay sprawled upon a bit of grass across the road, and to Dr Fenton's right, several doors northward, was Arnie's garage. He strolled up there feeling almost melancholy, found Irene Buford's car by simply looking among Arnie's wrecks out at the back until he found a recent one, peered at the registration slip attached to the steering-column, then wrote down the licence number, kicked a back tyre and strolled back to his own car, all without encountering anyone.

He hadn't been hungry in the village, but he had no sooner walked into his cottage where his housekeeper was in the process of making a pot of meat-and-barley soup, than hunger hit him hard. He went out to the kitchen, which he'd have done in any case to ascertain if there had been any calls during his absence, and Mrs Smith greeted him with the news that Mr William Carnegie was on his way to Concord to confer with Dr Fenton, and would Dr Fenton like to try the meat-and-barley soup?

He would. It was delicious. He forgot to tell Mrs Smith, though, as he pondered the reason for busy William Carnegie flying all the way out to the West Coast to see Dr Fenton. The mystery of this impending event, if it was a mystery, pleased rather than troubled Dr Fenton. He went off to the patio to read the morning paper, and had only just got comfortable when he saw a car heading towards his hilltop leaving in its wake a long banner of dun dust.

A patient, no doubt. He put aside the newspaper without any real regret. There was never anything very worth while in the things, unless of course one enjoyed having the wits frightened out of one. He rose and stood near the edge of the patio as the car wheeled up close and halted. A tall, lean man climbed out. Dr Fenton did not recognize him. He crossed over, offered a strong hand and said he was Joseph Aldridge, a New York private detective sent out several days ago to track down a man thought to be Basil Potter the Third. As though what he had been through this day were part of a normal routine, Eric Fenton took Mr Aldridge to a patio chair, asked if he'd lunched – he had – then stoked a pipe as Aldridge asked if Mr Carnegie had arrived yet.

Fenton lit up, puffed a moment as he studied the tall, lean young man with the curly brown hair and nice face, then shook his head. 'Mr Carnegie hasn't arrived yet, although when I got home a few minutes ago my housekeeper said he had phoned to say that he was on his way. *When* he will arrive depends upon when he left New York, and I have no idea when that was.'

Aldridge said, 'Five o'clock this morning, sir. He should be here after a bit. Perhaps you'd prefer I waited somewhere else?'

Fenton shook his head almost wearily. 'Right here is fine, Mr Aldridge. And tell me – what of the man with his leg in a cast?'

Aldridge's amiable look turned bland, as though he might not answer that question, but without being impolite. Then he shrugged and said, 'He's in Cleveland.'

Fenton removed the pipe. 'Cleveland? Cleveland, *Ohio?*'

Aldridge's smile widened at Fenton's astonishment. 'Yes, sir. He left Reno heading eastwards the same day he arrived there.'

'But – what's in Cleveland?'

'Well, I'm not sure, Dr Fenton. There was a woman but she left Cleveland a week ago and–'

'Wait,' commanded Fenton. 'By any chance, Mr Aldridge, do you know what this woman looks like?'

'Yes. I located a picture of her at the Bureau of Motor Vehicles.' Aldridge fished in a pocket. 'It's one of those driver-licence photographs so it's not very good but here it is.'

Fenton did not take the little photograph. He pushed away Aldridge's outstretched hand very firmly and said, 'Twenty-five, brown eyes, brown hair, quite beautiful, somewhat voluptuous, probably five feet and three inches tall and weighing in the vicinity of one hundred and twenty-five pounds.' Fenton then recited the licence number of the wrecked car down at Arnie's garage.

Joseph Aldridge listened, showed neither surprise nor great interest, pocketed the little photograph and said, 'Where, Doctor? Where did you see her?'

'She's in a room at the only hotel down in the village, where I left her recuperating from some minor bruises resulting from having stacked her car up against a tree outside of town. Her name, or so she told me, is Irene Buford. She is a single woman.'

Aldridge's smile returned, slowly though and a bit wry this time. 'Only one mistake, Doctor. Her name is Irene Potter and she is *not* a single woman.'

Fenton put the pipe back in his mouth, puffed a moment while he considered Joseph Aldridge, and eventually leaned back in his chair. It was very pleasant there on the patio; it usually was this time of year, with birdsong coming from trees round the cottage, with a faint low little breeze rustling the flowers at the edge of the flagged patio.

Being tired helped; it coloured a man's entire outlook. For example, Eric Fenton had never been a person who liked riddles. Now, he sat there smoking, relaxed, almost philosophical in the face of the greatest riddle that had ever intruded into his carefully ordered and deliberately peaceful existence.

Joseph Aldridge consulted his watch and thought aloud that he could probably go down to the village and see the girl at the hotel and return to Fenton's cottage about the time William Carnegie arrived, or shortly thereafter.

Dr Fenton offered no demurrer, but as he strolled out to the car with the younger man he had a question to ask. 'If the young lady is following her husband – Basil Potter – or if she is simply seeking him here, which I can understand since he worked as a labourer four days nearby probably to make certain the area was safe before he sent for her, then will you tell me how he happened to be someone named Floyd Merritt?'

Aldridge shook his head. 'All I can tell you about that, Doctor, is that he *was* Floyd Merritt all the way to Reno. I picked up the fingerprints on the bus he took up there. Where difficulties began to appear was a couple of hundred miles out of Reno.'

'What kind of difficulties, Mr Aldridge?'

'That is in Mr Carnegie's area, Doctor. I'm sorry. But he'll be along soon.' Aldridge slid down into his car looking slightly apologetic. 'But they aren't twins, Doctor, I can tell you that. And even if they were twins, since Floyd Merritt died eighteen months ago in Chicago, it probably was not him whose leg you set.' Aldridge gunned the car to life, nodded pleasantly and drove down off Dr Fenton's hill.

He missed seeing the predictable Dr Fenton break out of his philosophical mood, remove the pipe from his mouth and swear like a trooper. A man, even a tired, wrung-out man, could only be resigned and philosophical just so long.

Mrs Smith, seeing him from a window in the house, frowned, pursed her lips in strong disapproval of his language, and went scuttling out to her kitchen where no noises could penetrate from the patio.

How could this confounded brute with the broken leg lavishly distribute the fingerprints of a man who had been dead eighteen months all around Dr Fenton's examination room and in Dr Fenton's car, and what, in the name of all that was decent and right, was behind this entire episode of errors, where no one ever quite explained their thoughts, but instead seemed to delight in using mysterious metaphor?

Dr Fenton stamped over to his chair, sat a moment, picked up the newspaper, shook it savagely and composed himself through sheer effort to take up where he had left off when Joseph Aldridge came up the hill.

It was a total failure. He could not concentrate on the printed pages. Something like fifteen minutes later he was saved from having to continue the effort when Mrs Smith came to the patio doorway to announce rather pithily that he was wanted at the telephone. He got up and glared.

'No more sick people today,' he exclaimed.

Mrs Smith, who could hold her own in any company, glared right back. 'It's not a sick person, Doctor, it's a man named Aldridge calling from town.'

Fenton went to the study, picked up the telephone and knew exactly what Aldridge was going to tell him. He was correct: Irene Potter was gone!

Fenton said, 'All right, Mr Aldridge. But she will not have gone very far on foot.'

'She rented a car at that garage, Doctor.'

Fenton digested that. 'Still, she is not exactly ill, but neither is she entirely well, so if I were a guessing man I'd say she will not go very far. Bad headaches are very demoralizing, Mr Aldridge.'

The private investigator chuckled softly as he said, 'That's what I wanted to know, Doctor. Thanks. And will you explain to Mr Carnegie that I may be a bit late at the meeting?'

Fenton agreed, put down the telephone, curbed his urge to curse again, and returned to the patio, but this time to sit watching the southward roadway and not to bother with a newspaper whose news was by now nearly eight hours stale, and was not at its lurid best, as interesting as this affair Fenton was involved with against his will.

Well, at least up until now, against his will. Now, he was beginning to derive some kind of twisted satisfaction from the whole jumbled, nonsensical mess of it.

CHAPTER SIX

A FISTFUL OF ANSWERS

When William Carnegie arrived in a rented car, finally, he looked quite fresh. As a matter of fact after de-planing at San Francisco Municipal Airport he had gone to an expensive hotel, engaged an airy room, showered, changed his clothing, called downstairs for a car to be waiting, and had even had a light snack before undertaking the lovely afternoon drive up the coast and inland to the Concord vicinity. As he told Dr Fenton, when they met in the early twilight upon Fenton's patio, some day he would like to retire and live in this exquisite part of the country.

Fenton's recovery from that earlier passive variety of lassitude was by this time quite complete. He took the attorney into his house without a comment, offered him a drink, which was declined, then gave Carnegie the message from Aldridge, and derived some vindictive satisfaction from

Carnegie's astonished look. Obviously, the lawyer from New York had no knowledge of the woman from Cleveland.

It took nearly fifteen minutes for Dr Fenton to bring Carnegie up to date on Irene Buford-Potter, answer Carnegie's questions about both the woman and the missing private investigator, then point a cocked finger at the solicitor and say, 'Aldridge gave me reason to believe you know a good bit more about this entire affair than you've mentioned in any of our conversations. I believe the time has now arrived, Mr Carnegie, for you to clear the air.'

The lawyer neither demurred nor hesitated. 'That's why I flew out, Doctor. Although I didn't have very many answers until yesterday.' He looked around. 'Could I change my mind and have that drink?'

Fenton rose without a word, went to an exquisite mahogany sideboard, rummaged below the serving shelf for the bottled ingredients, made two stiff Scotch-and-sodas and went back, still silent, to pass one of the glasses to his guest. Then he sat down, leaned back and stared at the lawyer, making no move to taste his highball.

'Tell me about Floyd Merritt,' he said in a mildly gritty tone of voice. 'Aldridge said he died eighteen months ago in Chicago.'

'That is true,' explained Carnegie, after taking two swallows from the glass in his hand. 'Merritt was a mediocre hoodlum – nothing like murder or grand theft. His physical dimensions were exactly the same as the measurements for the man whose leg you tended. Merritt was a face in a crowd; he was a person who could possibly, and most important, believably, do just about anything from robbing a jewellery store to silently knifing someone in the back on the subway.'

Fenton finally took a sip of his drink. 'And of course there is a definite connection,' he said. 'All right, Mr Carnegie – what was it?'

'Basil Potter was not altogether engrossed in ancient Arabic transcripts of the Crusades, Doctor. He was Floyd Merritt, lifelong hoodlum with a solid and enviably authentic police record going back twenty years, fleeing to the Middle East under the alias Bertram Porter, to escape the U.S. authorities who were after him for successfully robbing an armoured bank-express lorry of three and a half million dollars. Doctor, there really was such a robbery. The three and a half million dollars actually did disappear.'

Dr Fenton swished his drink without lifting his eyes from William Carnegie. 'Are you trying to tell me,' he said dryly, 'that Basil Potter the Third is a–?'

'One moment, please,' said Carnegie, breaking in quickly. 'Let me finish. That armoured car robbery took place three days after the demise of Floyd Merritt. The Central Security Agency had seven men from one end of the country to the other end under close surveillance, waiting for one to die. Merritt obliged, in Chicago. All those seven men matched Basil Potter in every physical way.'

Fenton broke in again. 'Are you saying Basil Potter is a spy?'

Carnegie ignored the interruption. 'The incredible part was to make Floyd Merritt live again. It was done by elbow-length sheaths made from the skin of the dead man.' Carnegie finally paused, willing at last to be interrupted. But Doctor Fenton did not interrupt. He finished his drink, put aside the empty glass and searched through several pockets for his pipe and pouch.

Then he said one word: 'Why?'

'To spend as much of three million dollars as it was necessary to spend, to buy off Middle East *provocateurs*, Doctor.'

'Did it work?'

'Well, if you've been reading your newspapers the last month or so, I think you'll know the answer. It has worked.'

'And Potter?'

'A recruit, Doctor. A very capable and gifted recruit, but not a professional. According to my informant in the Central Security Agency they no longer use professionals in enterprises of this nature. They prefer people they keep lists of, who could bring off special assignments.'

Fenton lit his pipe, puffed, then sighed aloud and said, 'Carnegie, you ought to write books on science-fiction. Or something like that. Now please explain the woman.'

'Basil Potter married her over a year ago. He left the country bound for the Mid-East seven months ago. He returned, via London, where he reported in, four weeks ago. For something like five months he and his bride were together.'

'In Cleveland?'

'Yes.'

'And he got word to her he was out here, near his uncle's estate?'

'Evidently, although that's pure guesswork. She will probably substantiate it, when we find her.'

'I thought you were surprised when I told you about her, Carnegie.'

The lawyer shook his head. 'I was surprised that she was *here*, Doctor, but as of yesterday when I finally got the whole story from the government people, I knew Potter had a wife.'

'And did your government people tell you why young Potter would think his life was in danger?'

Carnegie replied almost casually, 'That was the easiest part. In fact, after talking to you about this stranger and his fears, it occurred to me that if he were not involved with, say, some outfit like the Mafia, then he probably was involved with some kind of government apparatus. I put out some feelers and made my discovery. The people who would like revenge against Basil Potter, Doctor, are the revolutionaries whom he scuttled by bribing their top men. The Central Security Authorities told me it was possible they had Arab assassins – rather like the Arab psychopath who gunned down Senator Kennedy – in this country, but so far they have been unable to ascertain absolutely that this is so.

'Why don't they ask Potter?' asked Dr

Fenton. 'I can tell you, from a professional standpoint, that Basil Potter is not an emotionally disturbed person. If he believes he is being hunted, take my word for it, Carnegie, *he is being hunted*.'

'Quite, Doctor, and the C.S.A. people are watching every move Basil Potter makes.'

Fenton considered his empty highball glass as though it were the only real friend close by. He asked if Carnegie would care for a refill and when the lawyer declined Fenton went wordlessly to get a refill for himself. From over at the sideboard he said, 'What does all this do to me? Potter told me he could not afford the kind of publicity accepting his inheritance would involve. And by God, Carnegie, I will not continue as the executor of that estate.'

'We have arranged a contingency plan,' said the lawyer, smoothly. So smoothly in fact that as Fenton strode back to his chair he put a caustic look upon his guest. He sat, sipped, and looked steadily at Carnegie, unamused but not far from smiling.

'We will petition the court for a change of executors. We will also petition for a transfer of authority to the legal heir, requesting a closed hearing, and my law firm will act in a proxy capacity after appraising the court of the true situation. Basil Potter will only have to make one appearance before the court, to verify his identity. Then Carnegie, Duff and McGregor take it from there. How does that sound, Doctor?'

'Very thorough,' said Fenton. 'And who will the new executor be?'

'Not an individual, Doctor, but an entire law firm.'

'Great,' smiled Fenton. 'The law firm of Carnegie Duff and McGregor. Well, Mr Carnegie, I've changed my mind. I'll stay on as executor.'

Dr Fenton raised his glass and drank. William Carnegie stared at him. He had never really understood Eric Fenton, so perhaps he shouldn't have been too surprised. Maybe he wasn't, because he now said, 'Would you explain, please?'

'I'm not sure that I can explain,' replied Fenton. 'Being that old fraud's executor and instrument irked me considerably. But I suppose helping his nephew, who evidently is anything but a fraud, isn't too much for someone whose schedule isn't too crowded these days.'

Carnegie looked approving. 'Good. It was a little more than I hoped for when I decided to come out and personally put things into proper perspective, Doctor. But I'm certainly gratified. I'm sure Basil will be too.'

'If,' said Fenton, 'he lives. And if he ever gets back here, Mr Carnegie, and if in the mix-up someone doesn't pot-shoot me too, before Potter can thank me. By the way, his wife is a striking woman.' Fenton drained half his glass. 'I suppose, Mr Carnegie, that some die young, and some die when they are not quite so young.'

Carnegie sat gazing at his host, possibly slightly puzzled by that last remark; perhaps he even attributed it to those two strong highballs Dr Fenton had consumed. He ventured a probing comment. 'Young Potter is a difficult man to make a hero of, Doctor. His uncle was somewhat right when he called him a wastrel and a vagabond.'

Fenton smiled and finished his second drink. 'Wouldn't we all love to be those things when we are young, Carnegie? And as for his uncle – he wasn't qualified to pass judgement on a mongrel dog. Since we seem to be dealing in anti-heroes, I nominate old Basil Potter as the all-American louse of his generation – with palms.' Fenton's smile slowly faded. He rubbed his eyes and said, 'I've had one hell of a day today. Can I put you up for the night? Got lots of room and rather like company for breakfast.'

'It's a frightful imposition, Doctor. I really should go down to the hotel in Concord.'

Fenton got none too steadily to his feet. 'Nonsense, man. Come along; I'll show you your room.'

Carnegie rose, gazing askance at his host. 'Are you all right, Dr Fenton?'

'Well, by God, I'd better be, Carnegie, because who can look after the doctor if the doctor gets sick?' Fenton boomed out a big, rolling laugh, hooked Carnegie's arm and hauled him along down a cheery little hallway to a bedroom doorway. 'In you go,' he said, shoving the door back. 'Breakfast will be whenever you arise… Good God, Carnegie, I think I'm drunk.'

The lawyer smiled. 'I think so too, Doctor. Good night.'

'Where the hell is that lovely girl tonight, Carnegie, and that old bastard's nephew? It seems to be that confounded National Security Agency fouled things up by not protecting him better. And say – can you tell me why he ever came here in the first place?'

'He knew his uncle was dead, Doctor. He knew he was the sole heir.'

Dr Fenton weaved over and leaned upon

the door jamb. 'Let me tell you something, Mr New-York-Lawyer: That young man couldn't care less about inheriting thirty million dollars. You wait until you've spoken to him. Then you'll see how right I am. So – why did he come here?'

Carnegie smiled gently. 'I'll see you in the morning, Doctor, and thanks very much for putting me up. Good night.'

Dr Fenton rolled on down the hallway to his own room, entered, shed his clothing from the doorway to the large bed, and sat down at last to shuck his shoes, acknowledging himself to be drunk for the first time in about twenty years.

CHAPTER SEVEN

SLEEPING BEAUTY

Neither Eric Fenton nor his house guest mentioned that awkward ending to their visit the evening before, and even if they had wanted to there would have been disconcerting complications. They were at breakfast the following morning when

Carnegie was called to the telephone by Mrs Smith. When he returned he looked rather preoccupied. 'It was Aldridge,' he explained, taking his chair at the table again and reaching for the coffee. 'He is on his way back here with the girl.'

Fenton cocked his eyebrows. 'Here, to Concord?'

'No, Doctor, here to your cottage – perhaps I should have said: Here to your clinic. He found her parked off the road a fair distance from Concord with her head cradled in her hands over the steering-wheel.' Carnegie frowned. 'Last night, as I recall, you mentioned a car wreck. I should have asked at the time: How bad were her injuries?'

'A headache,' said Dr Fenton. 'Upset stomach. The normal results of being in a car, behind the steering-wheel, when a head-on collision occurs. Except that she was more fortunate than most people, Carnegie. She either was not travelling very fast at the time of impact, or she was relaxed enough to yield when she struck something with her body and her head.'

'How about concussion, Doctor?'

Fenton's eyes narrowed. 'Why do you ask? Did Aldridge say she was incoherent or something like that?'

'Not incoherent, but he told me she was lethargic, sluggish, drowsy-acting.'

Fenton thought that over while Mrs Smith refilled their coffee cups. As Mrs Smith withdrew he said, 'How soon will Aldridge have her back here?'

'Perhaps half an hour.'

Fenton tossed aside his napkin as he rose. 'I'd like to see her.'

'Then it may indeed be a concussion,' said Carnegie, also rising from the breakfast table.

That nettled Dr Fenton; 'Mr Carnegie, I possess no psychic powers. I cannot diagnose at a distance.' He glanced at his wrist. 'If you'll meet them outside, I'll go to see that my examination room is ready.' Fenton strolled away, leaving his guest to amble his solemn thought on through the house and outside where a golden morning, and a high, distant fog rolling inland from the Golden Gate estuary, made the land in all directions seem almost unreal, seem too peaceful and serene.

He was still out there when Dr Fenton came from his little clinic looking brisk and businesslike except for the pipe in his mouth. Carnegie pointed in the direction of

Concord where a dark car was hastening northward. It was the only car in sight, which encouraged Carnegie to believe it might be Aldridge. It was, but neither of the watching men were certain of that until the car swung in at Dr Fenton's private entrance and came quickly up the hill.

Aldridge nodded briskly, climbed from the car and went to the far door to help the woman out. She looked dull and haggard. Her movements were not very coordinated. Carnegie moved forward but Eric Fenton reached the woman's side first. He steered her towards his clinic and when the four of them were inside, Fenton eased her down upon a sofa. He made a cursory examination, starting, and ending, with the woman's eyes. They seemed dilated, incapable of proper focusing, and fixed. Carnegie, who had noticed this, asked about its significance, and Fenton responded by ordering both Carnegie and Aldridge out of the examination room.

When he joined them something like fifteen minutes later, they were sitting out on the patio talking quietly. Carnegie looked up. 'Concussion, Doctor?'

Fenton dropped into a chair. 'No. Drugged dumb,' he said, and watched the expressions on his guests' faces remain bland. He smiled. 'I see. Mr Aldridge has already come to that conclusion.'

The investigator defended himself calmly. 'It was obvious, Doctor, when I first found her, that she was half knocked-out. Her speech was rambling and thick.'

Fenton nodded. 'But her condition, gentlemen, is the result of two factors that fool a good many diagnosticians in this age of drug use and abuse. In the first place, she is completely exhausted. I am assuming that is because she's been driving day and night since she left Cleveland. Whatever she's been doing, I can tell you she hasn't been getting enough sleep. To overcome that she's been taking sleep inhibitors. That's the foremost trouble. Then, probably as a result of her headache after the car wreck, she has taken too many aspirin. That's the second factor. That kind of combination will knock any of us out. But there is no concussion. In her own way she is stoned dumb. To you, Mr Aldridge, she would appear to be drugged, and in the technical sense that is exactly what's happened to her.' Fenton kept looking at the investigator. 'If you'd care to speculate further, it may make you feel good to believe that you may have saved her life. That road through the mountains has a number of very steep places where good drivers in full possession of their faculties have lost their lives. This young woman, in her present condition, would almost certainly have killed herself up there if you hadn't brought her back.'

Aldridge looked neither pleased nor displeased. He gave a clue about this, and also about himself, when he said, 'So much for that, gentlemen. What I'm concerned about is this: Did Potter expect to meet her at some prearranged rendezvous, and if so, when she doesn't show up, what will he do?'

It was a good question. Carnegie and Dr Fenton sat in the warm sunshine gazing at Joseph Aldridge. After some thought Fenton put Aldridge's question into proper perspective for them all. 'If he did intend to meet her, unless she achieves a miracle in the field of recovery, she will not be there. As for what he will do – I don't know the man well enough to make a prediction. But there is one way to get an answer: wait until Mrs Potter comes out of it and get an answer from her.'

Carnegie approved. 'When will that be, Doctor?'

Fenton's gaze turned sardonic. 'There are

drugs that could induce temporary recovery but I will not use them. She may sleep for six hours or she may sleep for sixteen hours, I cannot say, Mr Carnegie, so we will just have to wait, won't we

Aldridge did not accept this with the resignation of William Carnegie. 'Doctor, if she doesn't help us find Potter, someone else may find him first. But even if that doesn't happen, and providing the federal agents who are trying to keep Potter under surveillance manage to pick off the assassins, have you considered the possibility that Potter may return to this place? I'm confident he knows she got as far as Concord, and from what I've learned of him so far, I am also confident he'll backtrack to find her. If he does that, Doctor, he just may bring his assassins to your front door.'

Eric Fenton packed his pipe with deliberation, under two sets of watchful eyes. He lit up and blew a gust of smoke upwards into the still, golden atmosphere where it hung undisturbed until it had been diluted and dissolved. He said, 'No more drugs, Mr Aldridge, will be used on that girl regardless of the consequences.' Fenton's humourless, hard gaze drifted to William Carnegie too, challenging either man, or both of them, to a dispute on this point.

Neither man offered any argument. Carnegie even approved, but he didn't sound too pleased. Joseph Aldridge sat back in quiet thought, evidently adjusting to the altered situation. When he finally spoke he addressed William Carnegie.

'I telephoned New York last night, when the girl disappeared. They will send another man out. I think my best course for the moment is to do nothing until he gets here.'

Carnegie nodded. 'And after he gets here...?'

Aldridge gave a thin smile. 'It's rather pointless in a case like this to try and evolve workable plans in advance. I think, now, guarding the girl is probably as important as trying to protect Potter himself. And whether he knows it or not, he is already being guarded – but the girl isn't.'

Carnegie studied Aldridge a moment then said, 'And you think the girl is in danger?'

Aldridge evaded a direct answer by saying, 'If the assassins know about her, Mr Carnegie, I think it's reasonable for them to guess the man who loves her will try to reach her, will want to protect her. So she may not be in any direct danger, but if those assassins find her with her husband...'

Dr Fenton sat and smoked and considered Joseph Aldridge with an almost clinical detachment. There was no doubt about it, Aldridge was experienced at his work. And unquestionably it was interesting work. But orderly, pragmatic Eric Fenton, although capable of understanding the fascination such employment would hold for restless and active young men, foresaw no future in it, even if some mishap did not abruptly end an operative's life.

But then, Eric Fenton had always taken the long view of life: a man should have a profession, a stable, predictable future. Medicine, or law, or possibly something like the ministry even, that would always cover a man with security.

His reverie ended when Mrs Smith came to say he was wanted on the telephone. He excused himself to go indoors. The caller was a distraught mother whose son had sprained, or broken, his right ankle while playing leapfrog in the village cemetery using stone grave-markers as a substitute for playmates. Dr Fenton said he would be along after a bit to look at the ankle and meanwhile the woman should keep the child quiet and off that leg.

She said rather breathlessly that his father

was already on the way to Dr Fenton's residence with the child; she had only called ahead to be sure the doctor would be home when her son and husband arrived.

Fenton put down the telephone feeling annoyed. It would look a bit odd to the injured lad and his father having that lovely girl sleeping in his examination room. He went back to the patio, beckoned to Carnegie and Aldridge, called Mrs Smith to make ready one of the spare bedrooms, and took his male companions to the sofa where Irene Potter was dead to the world. There, gazing at the sleeping woman, he explained why he wanted to move her; then the three of them bent to lift her.

She would have been quite an armload for any one of them, but for all three of them it wasn't much of a burden. They got her to the bedroom where Mrs Smith was waiting, laid her down on the bed and departed, leaving Dr Fenton's housekeeper to make the girl comfortable.

Carnegie shook his head. 'She didn't even bat an eyelash. Doctor, it couldn't be some other kind of drug could it? That girl's as limp as a rag.'

Fenton led the way to the sideboard where he got out three bottles of beer, poured them into glasses and handed them around. For a man who normally drank very little, he was making up for lost time, now. He had a nagging little headache but he'd never have confessed having it after what he had done the night before; the beer might, as the old saying implied, remedy the headache, being 'a hair of the dog that had bitten him'.

He was also slightly edgy, but he strove to control that, so, although Carnegie's remark would normally have irritated him, he answered calmly.

'It wouldn't have to be drugs at all, Mr Carnegie. I've seen exhaustion make people so rum-dumb they couldn't remember their own names.'

Ten minutes later, while the three of them were sitting in the cheerful living-room with their beer, a battered pick-up truck arrived out in front of the house. Mrs Smith called Dr Fenton to the door as a darkly tanned, blue-eyed and shockle-headed rather rawboned man wearing faded work clothes, strode towards the house bearing in his arms a youth of perhaps twelve or fourteen years of age.

Fenton told Mrs Smith to take them round to the side entrance to the little clinic, and finished his beer. 'I shouldn't be long,' he said. 'And with any luck after this one there shouldn't be any more … at least I don't *anticipate* any more. But then I didn't anticipate this one either. How many individuals have either of you known who broke an ankle leaping over headstones in a cemetery?'

Aldridge and Carnegie smiled. Even humourless Eric Fenton showed a faint twinkle as he put the empty glass aside and marched out of the sitting-room.

CHAPTER EIGHT

SOME DIVERGENT VIEWPOINTS

If Dr Fenton had stopped to think about it he might have been intrigued over the incongruity of looking after a child's broken ankle while somewhere beyond his peaceful and sun-warmed hilltop a man he knew was shadowily seeking to evade killers, and a distraught, beautiful woman lay exhausted in one of his bedrooms, a victim of international politics, personal anxiety, and too much stress.

The farmer sounded embarrassed when he

explained how his son had injured himself. Evidently the farmer was a man raised in the old-fashioned traditions; they most certainly did not include playing leapfrog in a cemetery.

Eric Fenton scarcely listened. He made certain the injury was a break, not a sprain, and went to work to set the bones, and to immobilize them so that the processes of healing might not be thwarted by additional injury to the leg. Then he fitted a cast. He could have done it all with his eyes closed, or with his mind on something totally alien while his hands did the work.

The child was white as a sheet. He gripped the edge of the examination table as though expecting a blinding flash of agony any moment. Even when no pain came, he still clung there, expecting it. Only when Dr Fenton helped him sit up, said it was all over, did the boy – a tanned and rawboned miniature edition of the father – even begin to relax. He offered Dr Fenton a sheepish smile, then looked hopefully at his father. The farmer had a stern cast to his features; he evidently had not entirely recovered from the shock of hearing how his child had been injured.

The lad said, 'Thank you, Dr Fenton. I

thought it was going to hurt more than it did.'

Fenton had an observation to make about pain. He was of the opinion that the broken ankle just might have saved the lad from a good larruping by his outraged father. 'In the future, may I suggest playing leapfrog in the hayfields after the baler had gone by? I've never yet heard of anyone breaking an ankle leaping over hay bales. No pain that way. Well, all you can do, young man, is wait for the bones to knit. That ought to slow you down a bit, eh?'

'Yes, Doctor. Maybe, if I could ride my bicycle, I could come up here and learn how to tend gardens from that man working in the ivy patch down by the gate.'

The boy's father stepped over with outstretched arms. 'Come along. You'll not be riding any bicycle with that ankle for a very long while.'

Dr Fenton said, 'Just a moment. The man working in the ivy patch down by the gate, what exactly was he doing?'

The farmer answered, instead of the child. 'Looked to me as though he was planting tendrils by hand. I only glanced as I went by. I did wonder, as a sort of professional matter, Doctor, why he'd do all that with no tools.'

Fenton nodded. He wondered the same thing, but since he employed no gardener, he wondered more who the man was and what, specifically, he was up to. But this was not the place, nor the company to be in, when he asked about those things, so he escorted the farmer back to the soiled pick-up truck, reiterated to the father that the boy should not be permitted to put that leg to the ground for a while, at least until the bones were knitting, then he waved them away, watched them all the way down to the gateway where his private road intersected the county road, and after they swung right, heading in the direction of Concord, Dr Fenton turned slightly to the left and scanned the ivy patch down near the gateway.

There was no sign of anyone down there. He looked elsewhere with the same results. He then returned to the house and told Carnegie and Aldridge of the gardener the farmer and his son had seen, and who had evidently disappeared. He also explained that he did not employ a gardener.

Aldridge left the house and took a leisurely walk. From the patio Fenton and William Carnegie could see him stroll up to the ivy patch, then stroll right on past it.

Carnegie said, 'If there was anyone down there, Doctor, Aldridge will know it.'

Fenton's rejoinder was pithy. 'Interesting and dramatic, but unrealistic, Mr Carnegie. Rather like something one might view on television.'

Carnegie, up to now always polite, suave, even a little deferential, may have been suffering from his own case of rubbed-raw nerves because he gave Fenton a hard look and said, 'Except that on television gunshot victims get up after the cameras are off them and walk away.'

Aldridge came back, walking casually and with both hand in his trouser pockets. 'The kid was right,' he told the other men. 'Someone was there. But I think the farmer came up to him too fast, so he dropped to his knees in the dirt and began going through the motions of planting something.'

Fenton said, 'Who, Mr Aldridge?'

The investigator gazed dispassionately at Fenton as he said, 'I don't think that's the question right now, Doctor. I think what is pertinent is – where is that man right now?'

Carnegie gave a little start. 'The girl's alone.'

Dr Fenton still could not grasp it. 'For heaven's sake,' he said exasperatedly to

William Carnegie, 'this is broad daylight. Even if that weren't enough of a deterrent, he surely knows there are four people up here at the house, not counting the girl. What kind of a burglar would accept those chances?'

Aldridge smiled. 'Probably no burglar would, Doctor, but I'm wondering if those odds would deter an assassin.'

Fenton blinked at Aldridge, then said, 'Come along, we might as well go inside.' He did not add that by doing this they would be in a better position to hear any commotion if some intruder should actually try to enter the house.

Aldridge wasn't convinced this was what the stranger was lurking about for. 'He probably doesn't even know who the girl is. Or, if he *does* know, he probably means her no harm.'

Carnegie snorted. 'Of course he knows who she is, Aldridge. Otherwise why would he be here at all? You said it yourself, some time ago: Potter's enemies will expect Potter to back-track when the girl doesn't meet him.'

Aldridge said, 'Mr Carnegie, how would Potter's enemies know the girl was here, in Dr Fenton's house?'

'Well,' sputtered Carnegie, rummaging for a quick retort, 'Well – maybe they saw you meet the girl and followed you back here.'

Aldridge gave that thin smile of his again. 'Exactly. And *that* means they know Potter was treated here by Dr Fenton. My point being that *maybe* they followed me back here with the girl, and *maybe* they know nothing about Potter's connection with the girl at all – and have people spying on all the places they have tracked Potter to.'

Dr Fenton mulled that over. He did not say whether it seemed plausible to him or not, but he did know a way Aldridge's theory might be tested. 'Basil Potter worked for a grape-grower named Pete Silvera for four days. That was where he broke his leg – at Silvera's loading-shed. If these assassins think Potter will backtrack, would they by any chance also have someone watching the Silvera farm?'

'Very possibly,' replied Aldridge.

Fenton stood up. 'I think I'll drive over there,' he said.

Aldridge's eyes narrowed speculatively. 'I'll go with you, Doctor. Not that I doubt your ability at all. It's just that I'm trained in this kind of thing.'

Eric Fenton shook his head. 'You and Mr Carnegie will stay here and look after the girl. Mr Aldridge, maybe you're right; perhaps these people don't mean her any harm, but I refuse to take that chance.'

Aldridge would have protested. Even William Carnegie was having misgivings by this time, as he rose to confront Fenton. 'Let's wait a bit,' he said. 'I'm sure that if Potter is on his way back to Concord, the Central Security Agency people will be shadowing him. Let's not interfere for the time being, and when we know who is to be trusted, *then* we can play detective over at this grape-grower's place.'

Fenton, the pragmatist-turned-sleuth, declined to yield. 'What do we gain by sitting here waiting for someone else to take the initiative? I'll be back within an hour or so. Look after the girl, and if you need anything ask Mrs Smith, the housekeeper.'

For different reasons Carnegie and Aldridge wore glum looks as they watched Dr Fenton depart. Carnegie said, 'I think I understand now why old Basil Potter wanted Fenton as his executor. He's about as tractable as a steamroller.'

Aldridge's viewpoint coincided with Carnegie's, but from a different basis. 'If there is someone at this Silvera place, and Dr Fenton does something stupid, he could live to regret it – if he's lucky.'

Fenton's personal feelings, as he drove away, did not overlook the risk he might be running, but because he had time he could not make himself take this very seriously. It was a vague relevancy, a remote possibility that seemed melodramatically improbable, even a little absurd.

By the time he reached Pete Silvera's place it was noon. The packing-shed conveyers were silent. Labourers sprawled in shade to eat or rest, or smoke and make jokes. At the whitewashed old house itself, Silvera came forth at the sound of Dr Fenton's car and invited his guest inside to have lunch. Fenton demurred. He wanted to know if Pete had been troubled by loiterers. Silvera's response was to gaze with a perplexed frown at Fenton and shake his head.

'What kind of people do you mean, Doctor? Like the trespassers who come here in pheasant season?'

Fenton thought that over and nodded. 'Rather like that, but perhaps – well – just someone who has been observed watching the place. Like...' the word 'spy' came to Dr Fenton and he shied away from it. 'Like perhaps someone interested in what's going on here, or perhaps interested in your workers.'

Silvera sucked his teeth and looked away, over towards the idle packing-shed. He behaved in an embarrassed way, as though he wasn't too sure the sun hadn't bothered Fenton. When he looked back he said, 'No one like that has been around. In fact the only person on the ranch since you were here last is a man I hired to replace Smith.'

Dr Fenton was interested. 'When did you hire him?'

'The day before yesterday, Doctor. He was passing through and asked me about a job.' Silvera smiled. 'He's not a professional. I mean, he had to be shown how to pick and how to pack, but he is a good worker. Look, do you see the man in the new blue shirt, the one who looks like a Mexican who is sitting in the shade there smoking?'

Fenton saw the man, noted his rather sturdy, squatty build, and nodded. The man, at least from that distance, did indeed resemble a Mexican. The question that arose in Dr Fenton's mind was: Could the 'Mexican' be an Arab?

He said, 'Does he speak English with an accent?'

Silvera shook his head. 'Not many people do any more, Doctor. Most of them were born here. They talk like anyone else.'

'What is his name, Mr Silvera?'

'Like mine: Pete. Pete Martin. He doesn't pronounce it like the others; the Spanish way, you know: *Marteen*. He says it like we would pronounce it, Martin.' Silvera's dark eyes twinkled. 'It's fine with me. He could call himself Pete Nixon and as long as he worked good I'd be satisfied.'

Dr Fenton stood in a calm quandary. Listening to Silvera made it seem that Pete Martin was as harmless as any other transient worker. But he was the only new face on the Silvera farm, which was significant – possibly. If, on the other hand, he was indeed some kind of suspicious person and Fenton went over to question him, it might very possibly do more harm than good. He decided finally simply to return home and report this development to Carnegie and Aldridge.

He thanked Pete Silvera, climbed into his car and drove away. Silvera scratched his head in puzzlement, then went back inside to finish his interrupted lunch. He was not a man who devoted much thought to anything that did not touch upon his farm, his vines, his crop, the weather, and his family, which, when one considered it carefully, was quite enough to occupy anyone's thoughts.

CHAPTER NINE

AS THE DAY WANES

Carnegie and Aldridge were interested in what Dr Fenton had to report, but their enthusiasm did not include doing anything about the Mexican-looking man at Pete Silvera's packing-shed. They were both of the opinion that Carnegie's earlier attitude of waiting and being patient was the best course.

Mrs Smith fed the three of them, and later, only an hour or two before sunset, she came out to the patio where they were talking to say that she thought the young lady was getting up because she heard sounds coming from the guest-room.

Dr Fenton led the way. He was also the one who knocked softly on the door of the girl's room. For a moment afterward they heard nothing, then Aldridge gave a grunt as he spun away and raced out of the house by way of startled Mrs Smith's kitchen. Fenton and Carnegie entered the room by the door, saw the opened window and beyond it out in the garden heard an angry female voice. Aldridge had either heard something the others had not heard, like a window being cranked open, or he had simply guessed this would be the girl's reaction to having visitors, but in either case he had her by the arm out near Dr Fenton's bird-bath, which stood in the deep shade of a giant oak.

Carnegie also went out of the window. Fenton's dignity was bruised by this unorthodox egress but he followed Carnegie.

The girl had slept about eight hours. She still looked haggard, but that may have been as much the fault of her inability to freshen up with cosmetics as anything else. In her favour was the ire she vented upon Joseph Aldridge, who held her tightly as the other two men walked over.

Dr Fenton smiled. 'I'm glad you're rested,' he said, and introduced himself first, then his two companions. 'There's nothing here to fear, Mrs Potter. As a matter of fact this may be the safest place you've been in since Cleveland.'

The girl stopped struggling and stared. She did not say whether it was the name Fenton had used to her, or the name of the town in Ohio that had captured her attention. She looked carefully from face to face, then said, 'What am I doing here?'

Fenton explained. When he had finished, Aldridge had a practical thought. 'She's probably hungry.' Dr Fenton looked chagrined.

'Come along,' he told the handsome girl. 'Mrs Smith always has something handy.' He offered his hand to the girl but she ignored it.

'How did you know my name?' she demanded.

Fenton let the hand fall back to his side. 'It's a long and involved story. Why don't we go inside and discuss it? I'll tell you this much though; Mr Carnegie is a member of the law firm that represented your husband's late uncle. And I am executor of that estate. That ought to tell you we are not your enemies. Now then, shall we go inside?'

The girl yielded, finally, but Joseph Aldridge remained behind her on the walk over to the back of the house. He did not look as though he thought she might try to run for it, but if she did, he was back there.

Mrs Smith stared round-eyed as the men came into her kitchen with the girl. But Mrs Smith was not a very vocal person in any case, so when Dr Fenton mentioned food the older woman went right to work.

The girl sat down, when Carnegie held a chair at the kitchen table for her. She raised a hand to brush back a coil of hair, and looked pointedly at each of the men in turn. Finally, she seemed to loosen, to either accept the fact that she was not going anywhere, or else to believe Dr Fenton and the others were not enemies.

She said, 'I took too many aspirins.'

Fenton nodded. 'And missed too much sleep, and got half high on sleep inhibitors.'

Aldridge was always the detective. He said, 'Mrs Potter, when you don't meet your husband, will he come looking for you?'

The girl stared. She had met Dr Fenton before, but Carnegie and Aldridge were strangers. Moreover, after her tussle with the investigator out in the garden she seemed not too eager to converse with him.

Fenton played the role of friendly mediator. 'It's all right to answer,' he told the girl. 'We know the whole story all the way from Cleveland to Damascus and back to my having set your husband's broken leg.'

The girl started. 'Broken leg?'

Fenton nodded. 'He slipped off a platform at a nearby farm. That was how I happened to meet him.'

Aldridge looked with fresh interest at the girl. Evidently, if she hadn't spoken to her husband in the past week, or since his injury, she not only did not know he had hurt himself, she probably did not know he had been all the way back to Cleveland.

Aldridge said, 'Mrs Potter, where were you to meet him?'

She didn't answer this time either. Mrs Smith was partly responsible; she provided a perfect diversion by bringing a cup of hot tea and a plate of warm food to the girl. She also gave her employer a particularly antagonistic look. She obviously did not approve of three large men badgering one frightened girl.

Aldridge tried again. 'Look, Mrs Potter, we think that if your husband back-tracks himself looking for you he may walk into some rather serious trouble. What we would like to do, if possible, is contact him somehow and explain that you are safe.'

The hot tea and food helped. Irene Potter turned this entreaty by Aldridge over in her mind and after a while she said, 'He wasn't supposed to go all the way back to Cleveland. He wasn't supposed to go anywhere he had ever been before. We agreed on that when he telephoned me that he was back in the States, last month. We were to meet, yes, but not for six weeks after he returned. That was the C.S.A.'s idea. They wanted to give anyone who might be looking for him plenty of time to show up. The last place in the world he should have gone was Cleveland.'

'And you,' persisted Mr Aldridge. 'At the end of that waiting period, Mrs Potter, where were you to meet him?'

'Here, in Concord.'

Aldridge sat back looking at the girl. It was William Carnegie who came up with a new theory. 'Doctor, do you know what I believe has happened?'

Fenton looked uncomfortable. 'Yes, I think I know, Mr Carnegie. But I had no idea he was involved in all this. Otherwise I'd never have let on that I knew who he was.'

Carnegie nodded, looking unpleasant. 'In which case, Doctor, he would still be somewhere around here. Didn't it seem strange to you when he kept insisting he had to leave, even though he had a leg in a cast?'

Fenton's colour mounted. 'I've already

acknowledged my error, Carnegie. And yes, it did seem strange. I tried my damnedest to talk him out of it. I even considered having him arrested – as you will recall.'

Aldridge broke up this little argument. 'The fact is, gentlemen, he left Concord. But it's also obvious now that he will return to Concord. Doctor, apart from the man who was in your ivy patch and has now disappeared – but who undoubtedly is somewhere within sight of this house and this hilltop – there is that possible suspect over at the Silvera farm to worry about. If there are two of them here, there may be others. Tell me something, Doctor, is your telephone on a party line?'

It was not. As Fenton said, physicians could not be interfered with in this respect, so the usual rural multiple-use telephone line was not used. Aldridge excused himself and went out somewhere into the front of the house.

Irene Potter finished her tea, cleaned her plate, and when Mrs Smith brought more, the girl did not refuse. She was ravenous.

Carnegie drummed on the table and Dr Fenton dug out his pipe and proceeded to load it. 'Did your husband tell you,' he said, without looking at the girl, 'that he was being followed?'

She put down her tea before answering. 'He told me he *might* be, that he had told the C.S.A. in Washington he had seen a man in New York the night he landed back in the country, who looked exactly like a man he had seen in the airport at Beirut. He said the C.S.A. told him to keep moving, not to stop at any particular place, which would allow them to order their men to screen out any possible coincidences, and that when they had determined that he definitely was being followed, they would close in. He said he thought they should be able to do that before he got out here to Concord, so I should meet him here.'

She paused because William Carnegie and Dr Fenton were looking at her with the same expression. Then she spoke again. 'But if he wouldn't stay here, then he must have seen something that frightened him off. It looks to me as though the C.S.A. hasn't done such a good job of it, after all.'

Fenton nodded but Carnegie kept his own views about that private, and moments later Joseph Aldridge returned to the kitchen. He sat down at the table, looked at Carnegie and Fenton, then said, 'I have a friend with the Internal Revenue Bureau in San

Francisco. He ran Silvera's new man through the computers... No such man. The social security number he had to report to Silvera in order to be employed was a fake.'

Dr Fenton sat silently for a moment before saying, 'Aldridge, suppose I contact the constable down in the village?'

Carnegie, the lawyer, shook his head. 'In the first place, Doctor, your village constable has no legal authority beyond the limits of his town. I read up on California law on the flight out here. In the second place, even if he could go out there and make a citizen's arrest, which would be legal, wouldn't that simply alert any other assassins, and probably foul up whatever the C.S.A. people might have in mind?'

Dr Fenton chose to interpret all this as Carnegie's method of speaking 'down' to him. He said, 'It looks to me as though the confounded C.S.A. has already fouled things up. I'm *for* scaring off those assassins, Carnegie. I want Basil Potter alive, not dead. If we frighten his assassins away it can't possibly hurt *Potter* – and frankly I don't care a damn about the C.S.A.'

Joseph Aldridge moved in to soothe the feelings again. 'The man at this grape farm isn't our worry, gentlemen. He's over *there* waiting for Potter to return, and I rather doubt that Potter would go back there even if he still wanted a cover as a migrant grape picker – not with that broken leg. I think the assassin we have to sweat out is the lad who was in the ivy bed down by your gate, Doctor.'

Carnegie agreed. 'Potter will find his wife's smashed car. He will take it from there.'

Fenton argued. 'If he does that it's not going to lead him here to my place. All anyone down in Concord knows is that she was at the hotel, then hired a car from the garage man down there and drove away.'

Aldridge began wagging his head before Fenton finished. 'Doctor, that car she hired, as far as I know, is still sitting up there where I found her. It won't take her husband long to see it, verify the licence number, and guess that she either came back to Concord with someone, or was picked up by his enemies. *If* his enemies have no idea she came out here to find him, and he believes this to be true – where will he look next?'

The girl had been following this reasoning with interest. She answered before Dr Fenton had the chance to do so. 'Either down there at the hotel, or possibly right here, if he finds out I was shaken up when I hit the tree, and if he is told Dr Fenton is the only physician.'

Aldridge smiled across the table. 'Very good, Mrs Potter.'

Fenton had to succumb; his conviction that the labourer at Pete Silvera's farm was an assassin was not shaken, but Aldridge's contention that the *other* assassin, the one keeping Fenton's hilltop under surveillance, was the real danger, took logical precedence. Also, Aldridge's deductions about Basil Potter's probable course of action after he had worked his way back to Concord in search of his wife, seemed entirely reasonable. It helped to clinch that feeling for Dr Fenton when the woman amongst them, who probably knew Basil Potter better than anyone else, agreed with Aldridge.

Fenton looked at his wristwatch. Outside, the sun was still high although it was past six o'clock in the evening. He suddenly had a jolting thought. Supposing Potter returned after nightfall? How could he or the others know it was Potter and not one of the assassins?

He looked at the beautiful girl and said, 'If you'd like, Mrs Smith can show you the bath. Then you can either take a nap or join us in the sitting-room for more talk.'

Irene Potter smiled for the first time. 'Thank you. Thank *all* of you.' She rose and left the room accompanied by the housekeeper.

Dr Fenton frowned at Carnegie. 'Nothing but routine work involved in being old Potter's executor,' he said sarcastically. 'I believe those were your words, were they not?'

Carnegie nodded. 'They were. I thought all we had to deal with was a lazy wastrel. How could old Mr Potter have been so wrong?'

'He had a lot of practice at it,' growled Dr Fenton.

CHAPTER TEN

VISITORS

Neither Aldridge nor Carnegie mentioned going back to the village for the night. Dr Fenton probably would have protested if they'd mentioned it. It was Mrs Smith who brought this matter to a head by asking the doctor if he wanted to set the table for the young lady, the gentlemen, and himself.

He agreed that this should be done, and when Irene Potter came back looking very attractive, rested and alert, he made highballs for everyone. It was quite easy to act as though they were friends gathered for an evening of dinner, highballs and conversation. Beyond the windows lay a dark, warm night, and it was possible to imagine anything happening out there, but within the four walls of the cheerful, snug cottage one seemed entirely safe.

Carnegie went to freshen up, and after a while so did Joseph Aldridge. That left Dr Fenton, made warm and affable by the highball in his hands, alone with the voluptuous girl.

He told her the details of her husband's broken leg. He even told her how Potter had disliked Fenton from the start. She unexpectedly shed some light on that.

'The last time my husband's uncle telephoned him from out here, I was at Basil's apartment making dinner. His uncle tried to get Basil to come out here, with me, for a visit. Well, you see Basil and I were very busy at that time, and for a month or two afterward, and that's what my husband said. The old man mentioned you; he said he might send you to Cleveland to see what you could find out about me. That made Basil terribly angry.

Fenton looked surprised. 'Send me to Cleveland?'

'That's what he said, Doctor. Basil told me later his uncle said you were an employee of his.'

Fenton's amiability vanished. 'An *employee!* Why, that confounded old fraud! I haven't been anyone's employee since my days of residency after medical school. And I'd *never* have worked for your husband's uncle. I told him time and again that what he needed was a geriatrics specialist; I am a general practitioner. I also told him I resented being called up there to the mansion every time he had a runny nose.' Fenton paused for breath, saw how the girl was looking at him and brought his irritability under control. 'Well, the fact is, Mrs Potter, I felt sorry for the old pirate. There he sat, up there in that marble mausoleum of a mansion alone and lonely. I'd go up now and then of an evening and play chess with him, or argue politics with him, or listen to his stories. He was a wonderful story-teller, and what made his tales so interesting was that he mentioned the names of men we have all heard of or read about. But that was the extent of it.'

Irene Potter leaned back on the sofa with her drink beside her. She had only tasted it; evidently she was not much of a social drinker. 'Doctor, neither my husband nor I knew you,' she explained. 'All he knew was what his uncle told him. All I knew was what my husband relayed to me.'

Fenton understood. But there was something else he did *not* understand. 'Mrs Potter, when I was with your husband he not only made it clear he did not like me. He also left me with the impression that he wasn't delighted over inheriting the estate.'

The beautiful girl smiled at Dr Fenton. 'My husband is something of an idealist, Doctor. Money for its own sake means nothing to him. Also, he is aware of how his uncle made all those millions.'

'Your husband is a socialist?' asked Fenton.

The handsome smile widened. 'Not really, Doctor. I suppose if you categorize him you'd have to say he is a nationalist. Otherwise he'd never have allowed those Central Security Agency people to recruit him. He would wince if you used the word patriotic to describe him, but it fits perfectly. And, until we met, he really did not have any very solid objectives except that he believed in peace, and in our mission as a nation to ensure it. If he hadn't thought like that, Doctor, he'd never have agreed to do what he did for the C.S.A. As for his uncle's money,' the girl's smile faded. 'I don't know what he'll do with it, but I *do* know if he could use every dime of it to buy peace, that's where it would go.'

Dr Fenton sipped his highball, gazed at the girl with an expression of cynical blandness and said, 'Mrs Potter, take an older man's advice: Before your husband gets carried away, make certain that he invests at least a third of that money in some good, interest-bearing bonds so that you two will always have a healthy income – then let him piddle away the rest of it if he has a compulsion to do so. But speaking from experience, as a man who has seen war and the people who make wars, believe me, your husband can no more buy peace than he can run a foot-race with his leg in a cast.'

The girl's large eyes rested upon Dr Fenton's strong, unsmiling face for a long while before she said, 'Everyone has a purpose for being here, Doctor. It isn't possible to alter or scuttle that purpose. Maybe Basil can't do more than make a good, honest effort, but if that's his thing, then he's got to do it.'

Dr Fenton did not argue. He probably wouldn't have anyway, but Carnegie and Aldridge returned at this juncture, and moments later Mrs Smith came to say dinner was ready.

They had barely got seated in the dining-room when Dr Fenton was called to the telephone. Chester Crittenden, the hardware proprietor in the village, said his back was bothering him as a result of having lifted some nail kegs that afternoon, and he wanted to drive out and have Dr Fenton look at him; if nothing else could be done, at least to give him some pain-killing pills.

Fenton asked if Crittenden couldn't hold off until morning and was told that the pain had been increasing steadily most of the afternoon and evening until Crittenden could no longer sit or stand without being uncomfortable. He sounded distressed enough, which put Fenton in a bad spot. He did not know that anything was going to happen this particular night but he had a definite feeling that something *might* happen, either Potter would show up or the men seeking him would appear. Having

Chet Crittenden driving up in the night could be unwise. On the other hand he could hardly refuse to help the man. In the end, but without sounding very gracious, he told Crittenden to come along.

Then Fenton returned to the dining-room and told the others. Carnegie and Irene Potter listened in silence, but Joseph Aldridge uttered a sound under his breath that could have been a mild oath. Dr Fenton threw up his hands. There had been nothing else he could do but agree to see the man.

The meal was excellent. Most of Mrs Smith's meals were excellent, even the impromptu, casual little midsummer luncheons she occasionally threw together when it was too warm to eat. She was one of those people with an inherent ability. If Eric Fenton had thought of it, in the light of his earlier conversation with Irene Potter, it might have occurred to him that this was Mrs Smith's purpose: good cooking.

Aldridge was interested in Chester Crittenden. He recalled seeing a hardware store down in the village but that was all. Dr Fenton was brusque with his explanation because it annoyed him almost as much to be questioned by the private investigator as it did to have to see Crittenden tonight.

He had known the hardware merchant ever since he had been in the area, and he had it on good authority that Crittenden was a native from a long line of natives, Fenton's implication being that if Joseph Aldridge thought Chester Crittenden was some villain in disguise, he was emphatically mistaken.

Nevertheless the Crittenden affair cast a pall over the dinner. The other, more genuinely threatening affair might have accomplished this, although that was doubtful because of the inescapable feeling of security and comfort that permeated the cottage.

Then Crittenden arrived and at Aldridge's suggestion Dr Fenton brought him to the front of the house where the others could study him. Fenton did that, woodenly because it seemed ridiculous to him, then he took Crittenden round to the examination rooms and told him bluntly to climb upon the stainless-steel table, face down, and relax.

Crittenden's voice was muffled as he explained about lifting the nail kegs. Fenton's voice was distinct and sharp in contrast as he probed the man's lower lumbar area. 'You have to be a complete damned fool to lift nail kegs when you know perfectly well you do not have a strong back. How many times have you been up here for the same thing? I suppose, since it's a total waste of time warning you to be very careful, I'll have to use my alternative course to cure you.'

'What alternative course?' enquired Crittenden, face curled into the curve of an arm.

'I will henceforth charge you three times as much every time you come up here complaining that your back hurts.'

The hardware merchant groaned. It may have been occasioned by this threat or it may have been the result of Dr Fenton's rough probing. He said, 'Suppose I slip or something like that?'

'Unavoidable accidents – same price,' replied Fenton, and stepped to the washbasin. 'Chet, even without X-raying that back I can tell you one thing: sooner or later, depending upon how you take care of yourself, you are going to have to have an operation; perhaps a fusion.'

'Painful?' asked Crittenden.

'Very painful, Chet, and also very expensive. You are flat out for a long while, too.' Dr Fenton turned, towel in hand. Across the room a foot or so higher than his patient's prone, face-down form, was a small window that offered a view of the front patio, the driveway, and the black-topped parking area near the clinic. It was always kept closed, and on a dark night unless there were lights in the dining-room, as there were this night, the view out of the window was totally black. When Dr Fenton turned with the towel in hand, speaking to Crittenden, he saw a shadowy face looking in from that small window.

It was a shock. With the possible exception of Joseph Aldridge it would have struck dumb everyone else in the cottage. But Dr Fenton did not even noticeably falter either at drying his hands on the towel or speaking to his patient. Nor did he looked directly at the ghostly face. He gazed towards Crittenden, a foot lower in his line of vision, but concentrated on the sight within the fringe-limits of his perspective as he said, 'The fusion operation involves hours on end in traction, not to mention the business of carving you up. It's your choice, Chet! Use your head or have surgery.' Fenton tossed the towel aside. 'Sit up. I'll get you some pills. Tonight find the hardest mattress in your house and sleep on it. The floor would be even better. Whatever you do, don't sleep on your stomach.'

Fenton went to a cupboard, found what he sought in there, filled a small box with some pills from a jar, and turned. The face was gone. He blew out a long, silent breath, waited in case the face would return, and when it did not he went to a table, picked up a pen and wrote the directions for taking the little pain-killers upon the box. 'Incidentally,' he said as he went over to help Crittenden down off the table. 'Did you see anyone outside, when you drove up?'

Crittenden stood gingerly and accepted the pill-box. 'See anyone? Like what, Doctor? You mean like lovers parked on your lane?'

'Well, yes. Anyone like that.'

Crittenden adjusted his shirt, his trousers, snugged up his belt, and said, 'No I didn't. But I'll tell you one thing; it's that time of year again. Warm nights, lots of little lanes, and cars. When I was a kid only three or four kids had cars. Nowadays every kid has one. We make things too easy for them, Doctor.'

Fenton leaned against a wall-table waiting for Crittenden to get organized and depart. He wondered in a detached way whether he hadn't better warn the hardware merchant before sending him outside. He decided not to; if nothing happened out there Crittenden would spread the story all over town that Eric Fenton was imagining things.

Crittenden hitched up his tie, pocketed the pill-box and went to the clinic door. 'I'm much obliged, Doctor, and believe me if it hadn't been bothering me so damned bad I'd never have interrupted your supper like this. Good night.'

Fenton nodded, closed the door after Crittenden, then stood waiting and listening. He heard the car start, saw the lights sweep in a curving arc as Crittenden headed down off the hill, then he went to the other door, the one leading into the residential part of his cottage, flicked off the clinic lights and went to rejoin his guests.

CHAPTER ELEVEN

THE APPROACHING CRISIS

They took it well. Even Irene Potter, after one furtive glance towards the front windows, was composed and relaxed. She undoubtedly felt safe in the company of three men, two of whom, Aldridge and Eric Fenton, looked large enough to cope with any physical situation.

Carnegie helped himself to another highball at the sideboard in the sitting-room, under Aldridge's disapproving eye, and wondered if it might not be a good idea to telephone the F.B.I. down in San Francisco and see about asking several of their men to drive up looking the part of Fenton's patients.

Fenton did not even bother to scoff. 'How long did it take you to reach here from San Francisco?' he growled at Carnegie. 'If trouble is about to arrive a carload of federal agents aren't going to arrive here in time to do a damned bit of good.'

'Well,' said Carnegie, resuming his former position on the sofa near Irene Potter, 'how about weapons, Doctor?'

Fenton nodded. 'I have a pistol in the study, and one of these pellet-guns on the back porch. I've never used the pistol although it's loaded, but the pellet-gun I use as often as an obnoxious woodpecker lights on the house.'

Carnegie looked at Aldridge in mild dismay. 'A pellet-gun,' he murmured.

Aldridge smiled and probably would have spoken but the telephone rang. Evidently Mrs Smith took the call in the kitchen because the ringing stopped after the third sound.

Aldridge said, 'Doctor, I don't care if it's the imminent arrival of a baby – refuse.'

Fenton frowned.

Mrs Smith appeared in the dining-room doorway to say a man wished to speak to Dr Fenton on the telephone in the study. She did not mention a name and when Fenton rose, she watched him cross towards the study doorway with an expression of lively interest.

Fenton said his name. For a second or two there was no acknowledgement so he said it again, louder this time and irritably. He got a response, finally.

'Dr Fenton, this is Joe Smith. Do you remember me? That cast you saddled me with hasn't cracked yet. Now that the amenities are over I'd like you to answer a question for me.'

Eric Fenton had recognized the hard, deep voice at once. It had shocked him far more than the appearance of that face at the window. When he recovered he said, 'Listen, Mr Smith, you sound as if you're calling from close by, so take my advice and get away from this area as quickly as you can. Don't worry about ... anyone at all ... you'll know who I mean. There doesn't appear to be any danger in that direction, but you very definitely are in peril.'

Potter said, 'Doctor, if Irene is there she's in more danger than I am. I'm moving, but if she's up there at your place she's a stationary target – and they know all about her.'

Fenton, remembering things his companions had discussed earlier in the day, said, 'Are you sure of that?'

Potter's answer was hard. 'I'm sure. They were looking for her in Cleveland, but she was gone. By now they probably have found that abandoned car north of Concord. I had no trouble in finding it, so they won't. And that was the question I wanted you to answer: Is she there with you?'

'She is. So are some other people. Two men.' Fenton was fearful of speaking out as candidly as Basil Potter was doing, for some reason. He had an idea that he had to act this way. Later on it would seem absurd, but right then it didn't.

'What men?' demanded Potter. 'Police?'

'One is William Carnegie, your late uncle's lawyer. The other is – an employee – of Mr Carnegie.'

'Cop then,' growled Potter.

Dr Fenton asked where Potter was phoning from and had his question ignored. He then asked if he hadn't better ring the Federal Bureau of Investigation office down at San Francisco and Potter gave a curt reply.

'What the hell for? I've got a team of special agents around me like a mob at a bargain-basement clothing sale. No one's going to get through to me, Doctor.'

'I wasn't thinking of you,' said Fenton, annoyed. 'I was thinking of your wife.'

'Now that I know where she is, believe me I'll see to it some protection is sent out there. Doctor, have you seen anything, or heard of anything, that struck you as being out of the ordinary?'

Fenton mentioned the man at the Silvera farm who called himself Pete Martin. He also told of the face at the clinic window. Potter was definitely interested, but moments later, as though he might have been prompted, he terminated the conversation, leaving Dr Fenton standing in the study with a telephone in his hand that gave off the steady, dead signal. He put the thing down, went to a humidor, selected a fresh pipe, packed it without moving from the study, and lighted it. Then he returned to the sitting-room where three people raised their eyes to his face. He sat, looked at the handsome girl, removed the pipe and said, 'It was your husband.'

Neither Irene nor the two men made a sound. Fenton relayed the gist of his conversation with Basil Potter and paused once to tamp the pipe, to bank its ash, then he shrugged, looked out of the window, looked back and said, 'My impression is that Mr Potter is perfectly safe. All our anxiety on that score seems to me to have been thoroughly misplaced. But I also have a feeling that *we* are in danger.' He gazed steadily at Joseph Aldridge as he continued speaking. 'All your sound logic apart, Potter is back, does know where his wife is, has a bodyguard, and if those enemies of his intend to get at him they are going to have to do it in some way that won't put them face-to-face with his armed friends, the C.S.A. agents.'

Aldridge nodded gently. 'His wife.'

Carnegie tapped a coffee-table with his fingertips. 'If they are outside, Doctor, right this minute, what keeps them from breaking in?'

Fenton did not know. Neither did Aldridge but he made a guess. 'One man was in the ivy patch, and one man was at the clinic window. One of them might be able to bring off an abduction against the three of us, but if he had a friend or two success would be far more likely.'

Carnegie did not subscribe to that. 'He's had most of the day, Mr Aldridge.'

The investigator smiled that thin, knowing smile of his. 'I doubt that they had back-tracked Mrs Potter much before sundown, Mr Carnegie.'

Dr Fenton was sitting smoking. Now he glared at the other two men. 'Nit-picking,' he growled. 'Mr Aldridge, if you will put on Mrs Potter's dress I will drive you down to the constable's office in Concord.'

Everyone looked at Fenton. 'For what purpose?' asked Aldridge.

'To get them, assuming they are really out there, to follow us away from here as though we were making a wild dash to escape.'

Irene Potter was frowning in bafflement. 'Doctor, if you think Mr Carnegie and I could then leave in another car, I think you're under-estimating those people out there.'

'Well, what in the hell,' exclaimed Fenton, 'are we accomplishing here – beyond assuming the posture of sitting ducks?'

The telephone rang. Dr Fenton glanced at his wrist, then rose and strode to the study to take the call, because it was past time for Mrs Smith to be on duty. He snatched up the instrument and growled his name. There was no response, but more chilling, there was absolutely no 'live' sound coming from the telephone at all. He said his name a second time, then reached down to break the connection, and after a moment lifted his finger. The telephone still failed to respond. He broke the connection once more then dialled a random number, two random numbers. The telephone was dead in his hand.

He put the useless instrument back upon

its cradle and wondered calmly if ringing the telephone prior to cutting the wires had been to warn him, to frighten him, or whether it might not have been the result of some momentary short-circuiting of the ringing mechanism when the electrical current had been tampered with.

Whatever the cause of the ringing there was no doubt at all about one thing: there being no wind, no storm, no reason at all for those wires simply to disintegrate, they had been cut.

He went calmly to the study window, drew the curtains, went to the desk to dig out the souvenir-Luger pistol he had never fired, pulled out the clip to make certain the thing was loaded, lifted the top magazine until he saw the dull casing there, then put the weapon in his coat pocket. It sagged weightily. So much so he removed it and shoved it into his waistband, buttoned his jacket to conceal it, and, feeling absurdly melodramatic, returned to the sitting-room where, without comment, he pulled the curtains over the front windows then went back to his chair, sat down and said, 'The telephone is dead.'

It was like pronouncing a judgement. Aldridge said nothing, he simply gazed thoughtfully at Dr Fenton. Irene Potter neither moved nor made a sound. Carnegie said what someone almost invariably would have said.

'Are you sure?'

Dr Fenton did not answer. He rekindled his pipe, shook his head at Aldridge and said, 'Forget my wild scheme. We wouldn't get to the front gate... Mr Aldridge, we were babes in the woods. We should have got the hell out of here before sundown.'

'Why tell me that, Doctor?'

'Because, Mr Aldridge, you are the professional amongst us.'

'I see. And you think I've failed you. Well, Doctor, if I have you might remember I've also failed myself because we are in this together. As for running – it may surprise you to know that running in the dark is a lot safer than running in broad daylight. You make a more difficult target.' Aldridge slowly shook his head as William Carnegie suddenly looked interested. 'Forget it,' Aldridge advised. 'If the one watching the place has reinforcements, we wouldn't get ten feet from the doorway, night or not.'

Dr Fenton looked at Irene. She was being very quiet, understandably. She was endangered and frightened. Fenton could have smiled at her, showing signs of reassurance, but instead he sat there looking troubled, smoking his pipe, and thinking what a shame it was that such a strikingly handsome, and well-endowed, young woman had to be in this ridiculous situation.

'Car,' said Aldridge. 'Listen.'

They all heard it. It was probably still beyond the gate at the lower end of the private lane below the hill, but this was such a still, hushed night every sound carried.

The sound slowed, then picked up again. Dr Fenton knew that sound very well, people had been slowing to turn in off the county road for years. 'Coming up,' he said, and put aside his pipe, stood up and listened with both hands behind his back. Until he saw the way Irene Potter was staring he did not realize the butt of the Luger showed through the gap in his jacket. He blushed like a small boy caught stealing cookies, rearranged the jacket and looked over the girl's head as both Carnegie and Aldridge also stood up.

The car's lights, on an incline, bounced back and forth along the front of the house as it ascended, curved round to the wide parking area in front, and halted. Joseph Aldridge paced calmly to a front window and lifted the curtain. In a very calm voice he said, 'Maybe those telephone wires weren't cut, Doctor. Maybe there is something legitimately wrong with your telephone. Look for yourself; that's a telephone company truck and the two men getting out of it are rigged out like repair men.'

Aldridge turned with a wide, humourless smile. He had meant that only as a warning that the truck and the men with the truck looked perfectly legitimate as telephone repair men. 'Mrs Potter,' he said, 'will you step into the dining-room for a moment? Don't go too far, I'd like to keep you in sight. But just step through there for a moment if you will.' He did not add – so you will be out of the way – but his expression made that part of it plain enough.

The girl rose, pale and composed, and walked away. William Carnegie and Eric Fenton went over closer to Aldridge's window and peered out. Sure enough, two husky men in workmen's attire were approaching the house. Carnegie said, 'Doctor, if you don't know how to use that Luger, I do.'

Fenton unbuttoned his coat, fisted the weapon but instead of handing it to Carnegie he clasped his hands behind his back, facing the front door. He knew how to use the thing although he'd never fired it. With a thumb-pad he eased off the safety-catch. 'Mr Carnegie, if you will let them in, please,' he said.

CHAPTER TWELVE

A NEAR-KILL!

One of the repair men was a husky, stocky individual with a pleasant smile. He was younger than his somewhat taller, dark-eyed companion. As soon as they had been admitted to the house, the older man carrying a tool-box, William Carnegie closed the door behind them and Joseph Aldridge said, 'You are here because the telephone isn't working, I take it. Mind explaining to us how you knew there was trouble?'

The older man made a slow reply; first, he looked at the three unsmiling men, one in front, one behind, and the one who was speaking, off to one side, a slow, puzzled expression shading his face.

'Circuit-breakers are tripped as soon as there is a current feed-back. When one of our lines is programmed to accommodate a particular electrical load, and suddenly that power builds up and feeds back because it's unable to travel the full distance of the line, the tripping mechanism automatically breaks the input load and rings a buzzing system.'

Aldridge nodded. 'I see. But how did you know it was Dr Fenton's telephone?'

The repair man began to look a little annoyed as he also answered that question. 'No problem,' he said. 'Manual operators dial and plug in. It goes pretty fast. When they hit the connection that has no response they simply look up the address and buck the complaint to the maintenance section. Now if you don't mind we'd like to look at your telephone.'

Aldridge pointed to a table. 'Put the tool-box over there, please, and open it.'

The repair men looked startled at this command. The younger man turned. He evidently knew who Dr Fenton was. 'You in some kind of trouble?' he asked. 'I never seen these two guys around Concord before, Doctor.'

Aldridge gave Dr Fenton no chance to reply. He had one hand inside his coat as he repeated that order about the tool-box. This time, the older, taller repair man went to the table, put his tool-box on it, coldly and angrily opened it, picked out the top shelf so that the larger tools on the bottom would be exposed to view, and stepped away as he glared his frank hostility.

Aldridge asked William Carnegie to examine the toolbox, which was done. Dr Fenton too went over to peer inside. Neither seemed to have seen anything suspicious although it was reasonable to assume that neither would have recognized an electronic killing device if they'd seen one. But it was Aldridge's next order that really angered the taller, older repair man. His younger companion was simply astounded.

'Now put your hands on top of your heads and spread your legs!'

Dr Fenton saw the outburst coming and winced. 'As a matter of fact,' he said quickly, 'there has been some trouble here tonight.' He looked at Aldridge, who was waiting for the repair men to obey. He and the taller man exchanged tough stares. 'I'm sorry about all this,' Fenton murmured. But he did not attempt to negate Aldridge's command, and eventually both repair men did as they had been asked, but without ameliorating their looks of animosity.

Aldridge said, 'Doctor, Mr Carnegie, will you please see if either of them is armed?'

The younger repair man said, 'Armed? You mean, with guns? Mister, you're plumb out of your tree. We come up here to fix a damned telephone, that's all. And we're on overtime, so all this delay will have to be reported and–'

'Shut up, Frank,' growled the older man, who was being searched by William Carnegie and whose hostility did not abate although his stare at Joseph Aldridge seemed to turn more quizzical as the moments passed. 'Will you tell us what kind of trouble you've got here?' he said, to Aldridge.

The answer he got was amiable enough. 'Not at all. To start with, we seem to have prowlers. As for the telephone, we suspect the line has been cut in order to isolate us on top of this hill.'

The repair man said, 'Cut? On the outside of the house?'

Aldridge nodded. 'Very likely. Suppose your young friend goes out there to see.'

The younger repair man started to speak, possibly to agree with Aldridge, but the older man spoke first. 'Suppose you go with him, mister. I don't know what the hell we've barged into up here, but we're not buying into someone else's private war.'

Dr Fenton, the Luger beneath his jacket, said, 'I believe, gentlemen, that when you drove up here tonight and entered my house, you – bought in – one way or another. Either as what you appear to be or as something else.'

The pair of repairmen looked at Dr Fenton in silence, then the older one took his hands off his head without asking and dropped them to his sides. The younger man followed this example, but with a wary eye on Aldridge, who offered no objection.

The older man said, 'Beautiful,' in a soft tone of voice. 'Time-and-a-half overtime for making this run and we walk right into trouble.' He fished out a packet of cigarettes, lit one without offering the packet around, blew smoke, then looked at Joseph Aldridge as he said, 'My pardner and I will *both* go out there, mister, and you come along with us. Are you armed?'

Aldridge nodded, half smiling. 'I'm armed. For you or for someone else.' He jerked his head towards the door. 'Walk out ahead of me.'

It was Dr Fenton who delayed things by protesting, half-heartedly. 'Aldridge, you don't know what they might be prepared to do out there.'

It was one of those things a man might say when he felt danger without knowing quite how to cope with it, beyond adopting an adverse attitude towards facing it. Aldridge nodded agreeably at Fenton and jerked his head doorward a second time. Both repair men started moving. William Carnegie fidgeted, his face showing strain and anxiety. But he kept silent.

Aldridge was the last one out of the door. He slid a hand under his jacket, brought it forth with an ugly snub-snouted revolver in his fist, and closed the door after himself. Carnegie let loose his thoughts in a rush of words. 'If they aren't what they appear to me, Doctor, and get Aldridge – where will that leave us?'

Fenton didn't respond. He said, 'Go into the dining-room with Mrs Potter. I know where that metal tube is on the outside of the house. I can see it from the study window, if the moon is bright enough.'

'Hadn't the three of us better remain together?' asked Carnegie. 'You're the only one with a weapon.'

Dr Fenton said, irritably, 'All right. Then get her and hasten along.' He turned without waiting to see what Carnegie would do, strode briskly into the dimly-lighted study, waited an impatient couple of moments for Carnegie and the beautiful girl to appear, then he pointed. 'Go over there and be still. I'll turn off the lamp so that when I open the curtains I won't be visible from the outside.'

Irene Potter and William Carnegie obeyed. Dr Fenton, moving with confidence, flicked off the light, the dark-panelled study became utterly dark, totally silent, and Fenton pulled out the Luger again, no longer feeling at all self-conscious moving about with a pistol in his hand.

He stepped to the window, drew back one curtain and waited a moment until his eyes became accustomed to the gloom outside, then sought the little shiny metal cylinder with the wires entering at the top and leaving at the bottom. He saw the two repair men first, dark shadows gliding ghost-like in the pitchblende-shadows cast by the side of the cottage. Then he saw a third man, Aldridge no doubt, although it was impossible to be certain. The third man stayed warily clear of the other two.

Dr Fenton could not see the wires, only the metal cylinder half a foot or so above the head of the taller, older repair man, but he watched as the older man reached up, felt the wires, then dropped his hands, turned and said something quietly to Aldridge. The word was indistinguishable but the man's eerily starlighted face was discernible to Dr Fenton; it looked saturnine.

Aldridge moved in closer, the dark gun in his hand making black-shiny reflections in the darkness. The older repair man reached up again to show Aldridge something. That was when Dr Fenton saw the fourth shadow. It was coming in wraith-like and crouched, from behind the two repair men, from the west. Fenton's breath locked hard in his throat. He pushed the Luger past the curtains, felt for the window-latch, cranked it open and fired. For a thousandth of a second the whole world out there was brilliantly yellow-orange, then it was darker than before. The noise, bouncing off the back of the house, sounded like a cannon. Behind Dr Fenton Irene Potter let off a quick, half-stifled scream and the men near the metal cylinder were momentarily limned by muzzleblast as stiff-standing as statues, then they broke and ran.

Fenton said, 'Carnegie, go and let them in by the front door.' The doctor had never shot anyone before in his life. He had never even aimed a loaded weapon at anyone before. But as had occurred before during this most bizarre interlude of his life, the professional discipline of his vocation made it possible for him to think clearly and react to this emergency as he reacted to all crises.

He lowered the gun, looked back to where Irene Potter was scarcely visible, a hand across her mouth, then he looked out where the slumped wraith lay, possibly as distant from Dr Fenton's window as a hundred feet. In the front of the house he heard a door slam, raised voices, and the slam of booted feet as Carnegie, Aldridge, and the pair of telephone repair men came rushing into the study. By then Dr Fenton had arrived at his decision.

He cranked the window wide and stepped through to the ground. Carnegie and Aldridge started to protest. Fenton held up his Luger-hand for silence, turned and walked out to where that dishevelled lump lay, in that poor light looking for all the world like a flung-down pile of rags.

The silence was complete. Back at the window Aldridge stood, gun poised. Beside him was William Carnegie and behind were the repair men, little more than pale blobs in the night, but most certainly no longer looking as assured and antagonistic as before.

Fenton knelt, reached for the downed-man's throat and felt for his jugular. As he kept a pair of fingers probing for the pulse he looked around. There was no movement, no sign of anyone else, anywhere close by. But all that may have meant was that the downed man's allies, if he'd had any, were hiding, or had perhaps been frightened off by the gunshot.

The man was alive. Dr Fenton eased him over on to his back, heard rather than saw, the weapon thud against grass, picked it up, pocketed it, then slid his arms beneath the inert body and braced for the lift. The unconscious stranger looked to be of average height but he was a lot less than average weight. Dr Fenton rose with the man in his arms and started round the house towards the front door as though there were no danger out there at all.

Aldridge admitted him, locked the door, and almost before Dr Fenton had placed the wounded man upon the sofa, Aldridge had lifted the assassin's revolver from Fenton's pocket. He examined it standing at the foot of the sofa with Irene Potter, white to the hairline, at his side, while William

Carnegie, looking down from across the back of the sofa, watched Dr Fenton go to work with professional aplomb.

The Luger bullet had struck the swarthy man high in the chest on the left side, which was the side nearest the house as the stranger had stalked Aldridge and the repair men. The wound was hardly noticeable where the slug entered in front, but where it had come out at the back the man's flesh was torn and ragged.

Fenton made a compress of his handkerchief, told Aldridge to hold it in place so that the flow of blood would be staunched, then he went swiftly through the house to his clinic for some instruments, some bandaging material, disinfectant and an ampoule of morphine, then, as he passed back through the kitchen heading for the sitting-room again, he paused long enough to select a bottle of Scotch Mrs Smith kept secreted in the condiment cupboard, and took a long pull straight from the bottle before continuing on his way.

It had finally hit him, when he'd looked down into that slack, sweat-dappled face on the sofa, that he had deliberately shot another human being.

CHAPTER THIRTEEN

RAW NERVES

'Shock,' said Dr Fenton, as he worked swiftly, 'is Nature's anaesthesia. But like most of the natural physical defences, it is never adequate. In this case, though, since the bullet went completely through and the wound isn't too bad, I think we'll manage.'

He was correct. In fact, even after he had done all that was necessary for the time being, the slack-faced assassin remained unconscious.

The older telephone repair man said, 'Looks like one of those migrant pickers that come here every summer.'

Fenton could corroborate this; he had recognized the injured man the moment he'd stepped into the house where light showed up the stranger's features. 'He calls himself Pete Martin, and he was hired over at the Silvera vineyard a couple of days ago.'

Aldridge, who had verified that Pete Martin was not the man's name down in

San Francisco, looked with fresh interest upon their captive.

The younger repair man, the one his companion had called Frank, said, 'Mexican. This time of year we get an awful lot of them.'

Aldridge looked at Carnegie, then at Dr Fenton. 'You don't see very many curly-headed Mexicans or Mexican-Indians... Arabs, though, commonly have curly hair. Interesting analogy, isn't it?'

Dr Fenton said, 'Aldridge, suppose you give Mr Carnegie the man's pistol. That will make things a little more equal.'

Aldridge complied.

The silence closed in again, both inside the house and beyond it out in the darkness. Finally, the younger telephone repair man got nervous. He had been normal even after he'd seen the swarthy stranger shot a hundred feet behind him, but reaction, slow though undoubtedly it was with him, finally arrived. He stepped to a chair, sank down and looked forlornly at Irene Potter, whose colour had just begun to return. She smiled, probably because she recognized the repair man's symptoms, and said she'd go to make some coffee.

Aldridge dissented. 'You stay here –

please.' He looked at his employer, William Carnegie. 'Those wires were cut, out there. Now, the question is: How many are out there?'

Dr Fenton had a different thought. 'Where is Potter? If he tries coming here now he will very probably drive right into an ambush.' He began tidying up after working on the injured man. As he did this he thought aloud. 'I had some idea that these people would try to storm the house and take Mrs Potter hostage. It's been bothering me since sundown why they didn't break in.'

Aldridge had an answer to that. 'Why break in, Doctor? They don't want you or Mr Carnegie or me. They don't even want Mrs Potter badly enough to risk a fight to get her. They don't have to have her as their hostage anyway. All they have to do is sit out there and wait. If we know Potter will show up, it's a fair assumption that they also know it. So they sit and wait.' Aldridge gestured towards the shallow-breathing gunshot victim on the sofa. 'This one probably wouldn't have shown himself if it hadn't been decided they could not afford to let the telephone be repaired.'

Dr Fenton nodded his head about all this,

finished putting his medical things together on an end-table, and blew out a big sigh as he turned to face the others, and went through his pockets in search of pipe and pouch.

'It's like a B movie,' he said, looking from strained face to strained face, and finally dropping his gaze to the man whose blood had irredeemably stained his sofa. 'I don't even read the kind of literature that glorifies things like this. It's – just ridiculous.'

Aldridge gave that thin smile of his. 'Better come back and join the rest of us on earth, Doctor. It's never ridiculous when someone points a loaded gun at you.'

Irene finally went over and bent to use a piece of left-over bandaging to wipe perspiration from the face of the injured man. At her touch the stranger moaned. She jerked away as though she'd received an electrical charge.

The older telephone repair man, looking unemotionally towards the sofa, said, 'Doctor, you'd better get a syringe of deadener ready.'

Fenton put an interested look upon the repair man and got a little rough shrug. 'Served with the medics in Korea,' the repair man said. 'I've probably seen as many guys like this as you have.’

The wounded man feebly moved and Dr Fenton turned to the end-table to do as the former medical-aid man had suggested. When he turned back, hypodermic syringe poised, the wounded man opened his eyes. They were as black as midnight, but pain and shock probably would have caused some such dilation of the pupils anyway. When Fenton leaned forward the injured man’s grey lips lifted as though to shape an outcry, but no sound came and Dr Fenton drove the needle home, pushed the plunger and straightened back slightly as he said, ‘If you can hear me, please lie perfectly still. You have been shot and there is always some danger of a haemorrhage. Lie still, and in a moment you won’t feel any pain. Do you understand?’

The black-eyed man did not respond at all, but he kept staring up into Fenton’s face until his eyes closed again. Sweat made his dark face shiny in the artificial light. Fenton took the wad of bandaging from Irene and wiped the man’s face. The black eyes opened again and this time the injured man’s perception and focus seemed much improved. He drifted his gaze among all those strangers until he saw Irene, then he stopped searching and quietly stared.

'He'll get here. Porter will get here. He deserves it...' The man spoke quite distinctly but in a thin, somewhat reedy voice, all the while staring up at Irene.

She bent, took the wadding from Dr Fenton and wiped the man's face with a gentler touch. 'Which is better,' she whispered, 'blood or butter, war or peace? My husband doesn't want you or anyone else to die. Does he deserve to, because he doesn't want *you* to?'

The assassin's eyelids were heavy. He closed them, raised them and looked drowsily, rather glassily, upwards. '*Al Fatah*,' he murmured in a fading voice. '*Jehad!*'

That was all. The heavy lids fell slowly, and Dr Fenton reached a hand to pull Irene Potter back as he reached for the man's throat, probing for the pulse. It was there, rather surprisingly strong and constant in fact, but the assassin had gone back into his private darkness again.

The older repair man seemed to remember his job. He looked at his wristwatch, thought a moment, then addressed Joseph Aldridge, the one man among the others who had seemed most experienced and decisive. 'If there are more of these nuts out there, what do you think our chances are of getting out of here in the truck?'

Aldridge slowly and emphatically shook his head. 'If they haven't torn out your ignition wires I'll be surprised. What's the point in isolating us on top of Dr Fenton's hill if people can drive up, then drive away again?'

The younger repair man was recovering from his queasiness finally. He looked at his companion and said, 'How about leaving the truck and trying to crawl away in the dark?'

Aldridge vetoed that too. 'How about a knife between your shoulder blades for trying?' he asked laconically. 'For your information, gentlemen, these are not burglars or heist-men or car thieves.'

'Well, what are they then?' demanded the younger man. 'That one looks like a grape-picker and I've been looking at guys like him all my life around here.'

'He is not a grape-picker,' said William Carnegie with sharp emphasis. 'He is an assassin from the Middle East. At least he is a member of a Middle Eastern underground guerrilla army. You heard what he said a moment ago: *Al Fatah*. Don't you read the newspapers?'

The younger man did not reply. As always, when he was cornered, he looked to his older companion for aid. This time all he got was an exhaled cloud of cigarette smoke blown in his direction, and a dour stare.

Dr Fenton had only been half listening. If Potter came now, whether he came with armed C.S.A. agents or not, there was going to be a clash. He gazed at the man on the sofa, wishing the man had hung on long enough to say how many companions he had waiting out there in the warm darkness.

Irene Potter mentioned coffee again and this time Joseph Aldridge did not veto the suggestion, he in fact smiled and went with her out to the kitchen, which left Carnegie and Fenton alone with the two telephone repair men. The older repair man punched out his cigarette, strode to the edge of the sofa, studied the injured captive and swore.

'Damned maniac,' he said. 'Why don't they keep their stinking fratricides over there, where they belong?'

Either Fenton or Carnegie could have explained but neither did. Carnegie was examining the weapon he now had. It was an ordinary Smith and Wesson .38 calibre revolver. The barrel, once about six inches long, had been shortened to an ugly two inches. Serial numbers had been carefully milled off the weapon, which didn't mean too much since, if anyone really cared enough to make the effort and take the time, acid etching would bring them up again. Carnegie raised his eyes to Dr Fenton and smiled crookedly.

The doctor did not return the smile. He looked unpleasant. 'Nothing to it,' he said, needling Carnegie again. 'Just sign an authorization now and then so the old man's bills can be paid.'

Carnegie pocketed the weapon, shrugged and turned away. 'You'll have to admit not even the old man himself could have ever guessed anything like this could ensue, Doctor. Mind if I mix myself a highball?'

Dr Fenton said, 'Yes, I mind. Clinically speaking and regardless of those glowing distillery advertisements, I can tell you that even one weak drink impairs a person's judgement, perception, and reactions. Maybe you've never needed those three virtues before, Carnegie, but by God before this insane night is over my life may depend upon you having them now. No drinking!'

For some reason this amused the older telephone repair man. He was in the act of lighting another cigarette when Carnegie and Dr Fenton had their exchange. He grinned so wide he almost missed the tip of the cigarette with his lighter. Afterwards, he went over to the study doorway and stood there looking into the darkened room. Not until Dr Fenton, surmising something that might be going through the repair man's mind, spoke out, did the older man turn.

'If you tried splicing those wires now, they would kill you.'

The repair man's cigarette drooped, smoke drifted upwards forcing him to partially close one eye. He looked like someone who had just been told an unpleasant truth. 'What do we do, then, Doctor? Just sit around here and hope those nuts don't decide to kill us all anyway?'

'They don't want us. They want a man who is very probably on his way up here right now.'

'Fine,' said the repair man. 'And after they hit this guy, they just fold their tents and slip away?'

'They aren't going to – hit this guy – if we can prevent it.'

The repair man removed his cigarette, deposited ash in a tray and looked almost amused. 'Doctor, Frank and I repair telephones. We're experienced trouble-shooters.

But not your kind of trouble and sure as hell not your kind of shooting.'

The injured man groaned from the sofa, breaking off Dr Fenton's exchange with the repair man. The captive was perspiring heavily now, even his shirt was darkening. The older repair man came back, looked, and said, 'Shock is passing, Doctor. This guy's going to need a knock-out shot in a minute, or he'll come up off that couch like a tiger.'

For Fenton, whose irascibility had not been improved by all he'd been through this night, that casual remark was a waved red flag. 'Thank you so much,' he exclaimed, wrath and weighty sarcasm intermingled in his words. 'Maybe you'd like to prescribe the dosage and give the injection.'

The repair man raised wise, hard eyes, seemed to be considering a rejoinder, then shrugged and looked away as Aldridge and Irene Potter came from the kitchen, she carrying cups and Aldridge carrying the aromatic coffee pot. There had to be some good moments in the worst situations. This was one of them. Aromatic, good hot coffee to remind people they were alive.

CHAPTER FOURTEEN

A NEED FOR ACTION

The second hardest aspect of not knowing was waiting. It would not occur to Fenton, Carnegie nor Aldridge, until much later, that at least they were fortunate in having unwitting allies, the repair men, who did not panic or make themselves obnoxious.

As far as Irene Potter was concerned, she had been living with uncertainty a long while. That may not have made it any easier to bear, but at least she did not have any tearful nor agitated outbreaks.

The six of them sat, drank coffee, and when the older repair man finally said he would like to know what it was all about, seeing that his life was in danger as a result of whatever he had innocently walked into, Dr Fenton explained, with an occasional remark from Aldridge and Carnegie. When the explanation was finished the repair man finished his coffee, smiled at the younger man beside him, and said, 'Just like a Bogart movie, eh Frank?'

'What kind of a movie?' asked Frank.

The older man looked disgusted. 'Forget it. Drink your coffee and forget it, Frank.' He then smiled at Irene. Knowing the facts seemed to make a change in him. It was quite possible that before, he wasn't convinced he hadn't stumbled into an asylum for the mildly psychotic. 'It's a heroic thing your husband did, Mrs Potter, only I'm sort of an isolationist. I've been overseas with the army. I've seen conditions there, and take my word for it, there isn't any one country on earth, even the richest one the world's ever known, can do a darn bit of good for people who have never really helped themselves and are too childish to help themselves now. In my view, we ought to get the hell out and keep the hell out.'

William Carnegie said, 'The new isolationism. It's an enticing philosophy. Imagine how much richer we'd be if we withdrew all foreign aid, got our troops out, and sat down comfortably behind our nice big nuclear curtain.'

The repair man looked steadily at Carnegie as he said, 'And what's wrong with that?'

Carnegie blandly smiled. 'Nothing. Except

that our enemies would then infiltrate that much closer to our shores, and the next time we got involved in a police action it would probably be on the beaches of California or the border-deserts of Texas. But of course we wouldn't be so far from home then, would we? No chance to get homesick.'

Carnegie went over to refill his coffee cup. Aldridge was smiling at the repair man. It was Dr Fenton, who had been reading this endless argument in news magazines for years, who prevented it from continuing now. 'I've been trying to think of a way we could warn Potter,' he said.

Aldridge was sanguine about that. 'He'll know, you can bet on that.'

The telephone rang. Everyone froze in astonishment, but particularly the repair men. It rang again. Dr Fenton roused himself and went to the study to answer it. Behind him trooped Joseph Aldridge and William Carnegie. Neither of the repair men left their seats in the parlour, and Irene got the coffee pot to refill the younger repair man's coffee cup.

The caller had an incisive, crisp way of speaking. Under normal circumstances Eric Fenton would have admired the man's objective and oral clarity. After years of living among country people Fenton could truly appreciate good articulation and clear perspectives.

'I would like to know the condition of the young man you carried inside the house,' said the caller, 'and I want you to know that you and most of the others in there with you are not involved in any of this, Dr Fenton, so if you will do everything that can be done for the young man, you will not be harmed.'

Fenton stifled an urge to call upon the speaker to identify himself. Instead, he said, 'The young man is sleeping at present. His wound is bad but not necessarily fatal. I'm keeping him sedated and with moderate care and co-operation I'm quite sure he'll pull through. As for not being involved, I don't understand how you can say that. We are prisoners in my house. That's hardly non-involvement.'

The crisp voice said, 'Doctor, you are an intelligent man. You know what I mean. As long as none of you try to leave, to warn Porter, to go for help, you are in no danger even though it was one of you who shot the young man.'

'And if he hadn't been shot,' said Fenton with some spirit, 'what would he have done to those men he was stalking?'

'Captured them if he could, Doctor.'

'Yes. And killed them if he couldn't capture them. Look, suppose the man you are waiting for doesn't show up here tonight? You can't keep this house isolated indefinitely. In broad daylight patients of mine will drive up for medical treatment and–'

'Save your breath, Doctor. By tomorrow when your patients start arriving, all this will be just a memory. You see, we know that Porter is on his way.' The crisp voice paused, then went on. 'Doctor, if you are a prudent man you won't make an issue of this, particularly where the woman is concerned. If she gets frantic and rushes out – or if any of the others try anything foolish, *then* you will be involved. So just stay indoors, take good care of the wounded man – much of what we do after we've settled with Porter will depend upon that – and relax, Doctor, just relax.'

The telephone went dead in Eric Fenton's hand. He looked at it, then dropped it and went quickly to the window to pull aside a curtain and look out. He could see the shiny metal cylinder on the side of the house but he could not see the wires at either end of it. He turned back.

'Very professional. I should have suspected it. There had to be one of them at the splice. The moment our conversation terminated, he cut those damned wires again.'

Aldridge also went to look out of the window. So did Carnegie. Dr Fenton went behind his desk, sat a moment, then suddenly remembered something, pawed through desk drawers until he found the torch he sought, and with that in hand he returned to the window. Under the thin bright beam of the torch they could all very clearly see where the wires had been cut that second time.

Aldridge swore. Carnegie wanted to know what the man had said, whether he had identified himself, and what he had sounded like. Dr Fenton, torch pocketed, walked back to the sitting-room before he recited the highlights of that exchange, and he did so as he got another cup of coffee.

Everyone listened closely but Irene Potter picked something out Fenton and Carnegie and Aldridge had overlooked. 'If they call my husband Porter instead of Potter, they cannot know who he really is.'

No one commented although Carnegie looked as though he might for a moment, but Dr Fenton distracted him with a flourish of the torch. 'Any one of you know semaphore? Flash a signal from the front window using this flashlight.'

Joseph Aldridge laughed. 'Very good, Doctor.' He held out his hand for the torch. 'I was a signal officer in the navy for several years. I'll be a bit rusty, but then we won't have to transcribe a dictionary, will we?'

'You probably wouldn't get the chance,' said the older repair man. 'And how do you know when you start flashing the letters those nuts out there won't decide that's hostile action and bust in here to slit all our throats?'

'Or,' added the younger repair man, 'how do you know this guy Porter, or whatever his name is, will even see it? You guys could get us all killed for nothing.'

Dr Fenton was annoyed. 'Do you think we ought to just sit here?'

'That's what the man said, isn't it?' replied the younger repair man. 'Just sit here and mind our own business until this mess is over with.'

Irene Potter looked amazed. 'You don't want to help my husband?' she asked, her voice free of every emotion but genuine surprise.

The younger repair man looked at his

companion. It was the older man, looking at the girl, who dropped his eyes first, then fished out his limp cigarette packet and lit one before saying, 'Okay, but if we could reach the truck I could think of a better way out of this.'

Aldridge was interested. 'How? What's in the truck?'

'Portable transmitter that operates off the truck battery for emergencies. If we could get out there, even if those nuts have cut the ignition wires, we could still call in the cops. It'd work a lot better than using a flashlight everyone's going to see flashing out its Morse code for five miles.'

No one spoke for a moment. Evidently everyone was engrossed by the same thought: how to reach the truck. Joseph Aldridge finally shook his head. 'There isn't any way. Like you said, they'll see the light-flashes, but at least I may be able to get off enough of the message to warn Potter before they do something. But they'll be watching that truck. They'll be watching every door out of this cottage too.'

The repair man said, 'Every window too?'

Aldridge studied the older man. 'Probably. They wouldn't need an army to do that.' He suddenly gave that thin, sardonic smile of his. 'Are you volunteering?'

The repair man smoked and squinted at Aldridge as though he considered those last three words a challenge. It was Frank, the younger man, who said, 'Lay off, Bert,' to the older repair man. 'He's just trying to bait you. What's the point, this isn't our hassle anyway.'

Aldridge and the older repair man kept looking at one another, cigarette smoke hanging in the air between them. Then the man called Bert spoke.

'Okay, signalman, go and play with the torch at the window and while you're doing that I'll see what I can do.' He leaned over to kill his cigarette. 'One of you guys can hand over a gun, though. I'm not dropping out of a window into some damned flowerbed occupied by a lunatic with a gun in his hand, and me with nothing but a rosary.'

William Carnegie's reaction was the same as before, when some innovation had been mentioned. 'I don't think we ought to divide our force like this, gentlemen. I feel confident that when Potter arrives he'll have the C.S.A. men with him, and they certainly will have appraised the situation and be prepared.'

Dr Fenton looked down his nose at Carnegie. 'How does one prepare for an ambush, Carnegie, when one only thinks it might exist? All the careful skulking in the world may only allow one to walk right into it.'

Irene Potter, listening intently, seemed favourably impressed by Fenton's argument. But of course she had the strongest motive for bias on earth – love.

Joseph Aldridge held the torch downward and tested both its power, which was brightly adequate, and the sensitivity of its flash-button. He smiled once as he ran two Morse signals together, backed up and tried again. 'It's been a long time,' he murmured, as though the others had seen that error. He finally worked the flashes into readable dots and dashes, quite slowly, and spelled out each word as he went along. 'H-o-u-s-e s-u-r-r-o-u-n-d-e-d. A-m-b-u-s-h.' He looked up enquiringly. 'Enough?' he asked, then answered his own question. 'If I get that much transmitted...' He stood up without finishing the sentence. 'Mr Carnegie, if you'll give Bert your pistol.'

Carnegie reluctantly obeyed. He afterwards shot a swift, sideways glance over at the sideboard where Dr Fenton had mixed their drinks hours earlier. But whatever his thoughts he kept them to himself.

The older repair man, the one called Bert, stood up and examined the revolver. 'They must get their weapons from a junk dealer,' he growled. 'This thing is older than I am.' He swung the cylinder out, spun it, flicked it back and checked the cocking and safety mechanisms. 'It's better than a fly-swatter,' he said, and smiled a bit bleakly at Aldridge. 'Which is the best way out – and don't drop me against a white wall with no cover.'

Frank was troubled. 'Listen to me,' he said fervently. 'We don't get paid for this kind of stuff, Bert. You've got to be out of your skull. This isn't our fight.'

Bert looked down. 'I don't know whether it is or not, Frank, but I've got a kind of feeling it may be. Well, that doesn't make much sense does it?' He smiled at the younger repair man. 'Hang in there, Frank. Do what your mother taught you to do – pray.' He raised his face with the smile fading and looked past Aldridge to Dr Fenton. 'You'd know which window I've got to get out of, Doctor. Where there's plenty of cover outside and where it's dark and maybe they won't be looking. You got something like that?'

Eric Fenton nodded. 'Off the pantry. But frankly, I'm having second thoughts about your involvement.'

Bert smiled. 'So am I, so let's get cracking before I bug out.' He looked at Aldridge. 'You'd better get to making with the flashlight, signalman.'

Aldridge nodded. Those two looked squarely at one another briefly, then the repair man said, 'Come on, Doctor,' and started walking towards the empty, dark and silent dining-room.

Fenton looked a little upset, but he went along. Someone, he bitterly promised himself, was going to answer for all this, later.

CHAPTER FIFTEEN

A DEGREE OF SUCCESS

The pantry was between the dining-room and kitchen. Beyond it, in a jutting northerly wing of the cottage, Mrs Smith, the housekeeper, was blissfully slumbering. Her room was what gave the pantry window its protection from starlight after the close of day. It also shaded the pantry window from direct sunshine. This factor had inspired the planting of luxuriant, jungle-like flora including a bank of magnificent roses, three dwarf orange trees – elsewhere the occasional winter frosts would have killed them – and a hedge of flourishing elephant-ear which, if it had any aesthetic beauty at all, it had to be in the eye of some biased observer, like Eric Fenton, because apart from elephantine leaves that sagged and were a sickly pale shade of green, the plants neither flowered nor offered an acceptable perfume.

They did, however, justify all the years of their rather hit-and-miss care by Eric Fenton on this particular night. When the window was open and the repair man had leaned out for a long time looking, trying to sense what might be beyond in the darkness, he leaned back and said in a whisper he thought he could make it, that the cover was perfect and there did not seem to be anyone around. Nevertheless, he said in admonition, Dr Fenton was to stand in that damned window with his Luger off-safety to give cover-fire if it should prove necessary.

Fenton nodded and offered a hand. The repair man looked down, looked up and said, ‘Doctor, I’m not going to heaven or a hospital. I’ll be back.’ He did not shake the offered hand. He got on top of a shelf just below the window, eased out and dropped soundlessly into the flower bed below. It was possible to see the telephone company’s panel truck up along the side of the house. As Dr Fenton watched, the repair man began inching his way forward.

Fenton was sure the man would be safe enough until he reached the front of the house. Between the landscaping at the corner of the cottage, and the truck on across the black-topped driveway, there was not so much as a blade of grass. Moreover, by now Aldridge would be getting some attention from the hidden assassins, and that would also be in front where the flashes of light would be visible from the distant county road.

Dr Fenton closed and locked the pantry window, took up his Luger and went back into the dining-room. Here, he could see the driveway, the truck and parking area, as well as the nearby corner of the converging walls where the repair man would eventually arrive. He parted the curtain very gently, reached beyond to crank the window open just a bit, then he tried to look to his right, along the front of the house, and detect flashes of light.

There were none. He looked closer, then swore to himself and stepped to the sitting-room entranceway. The young repair man was slouched on the sofa, looking both apprehensive and sulky. Irene and William Carnegie were also there, glum and rather dejected looking. Dr Fenton hissed at them.

'Where is Aldridge?'

Carnegie pointed. 'In that corner bed-room that looks down towards the road and the village.' Carnegie started to spring to his feet, as though he thought something had gone wrong. 'What is it, Doctor?'

Fenton was so relieved he smiled. 'Nothing. Just sit back down and relax. I couldn't see the flashes, that is all.'

Aldridge had done the best thing. Not only would his signal be more readily visible in the direction of Concord, but it would also draw whatever enemy attention it might attract over to the farthest corner of the front of the house; actually, over to the south side of the house. The front of the cottage faced east. That was why Fenton smiled.

He returned to the dining-room window, evinced a little boldness by drawing the curtain farther aside and cranking open the window a bit more, so that he could peer down and to his left, to the shrubbery at the corner of the house.

He did not see the repair man, not at first, although he saw some faint, quick movement in the bushes which meant the man was getting close.

Then he saw the repair man; part of his face and part of one dark shoulder eased ahead. He looked along the front of the house, took his time ascertaining there was no sign of trouble along there, and eventually turned to study the truck on ahead. He remained like that, kneeling, totally still, for so long Dr Fenton wondered if he had seen something. Fenton also looked over to where the truck stood in ghostly night-light. At first he saw only a harmless light lorry, but after a moment he saw what he thought must have caught and held the repair man's attention. A blurry round object looking down towards the southerly corner of the house *from inside the lorry!*

Fenton's irascibility prompted him to form several blistering curses with his lips. Exasperation made him almost angry enough to do something rash, but not quite. Bert the repair man still squatted there but Eric Fenton anticipated his withdrawal back to the pantry window. Even if he could get across the open parking area unseen, he couldn't possibly get inside the repair man's van without attracting the attention of the man already inside.

Someone whistled. It sounded as though it were southward and a long way off. Dr Fenton swung back, sure that Aldridge's flashes had been detected. He glimpsed a fleet shadow passing towards the far corner of the front of the cottage, hugging in close so as to avoid detection until the last possible moment. Something in the opposite direction distracted him, a slight, sighing sound. He looked around and down again. Bert the repair man was not there. He almost sprang back to hasten to the pantry window, then a vague blur north of the parked lorry and near a pomegranate bush caught his attention anew. This time he could make out the dark-suited silhouette as it passed almost rashly along until it was even with the van. From this direction, the distance to be crossed without protection was no more than perhaps forty to sixty feet. Obviously Bert was attempting to take fullest advantage of the diversion to the south.

He pushed through the pomegranate

bush, crouched low and started swiftly padding across towards the van. Dr Fenton saw white, and realized suddenly that Bert had left his shoes behind before stepping upon the pavement. He would have admired that tactic if he'd had the time.

Bert got to the side of his van and was lost to Dr Fenton because of the position of the vehicle and also because of the distance and darkness. The Luger was slippery in his fist. He shifted it to the other hand and dried his palm down a trouser-leg. A crashing sound of smashed glass made him jump. Someone, at the opposite end of the house, had either put Aldridge's flashlight out of commission or had broken the window in front of Aldridge.

Fenton turned quickly back towards the van. There was not a sign of activity over there, outside or inside. He squinted hard trying to detect that shadowy face inside, and failed. For a full sixty seconds he waited, attuned to sound or sight or movement, and detected nothing at all.

He rested the Luger upon a sill and leaned cautiously to peer southward. There were no flashes of light down there. There was no sound or movement in that direction either. A whisper of sound at his back made him whirl, Luger raised. It was William Carnegie to whisper that the assassins had put Aldridge out of commission with a lead pellet through his lower arm. The flashlight was broken, Carnegie said forlornly, and looked at the opened window as he said, 'You'd better come and have a look at Aldridge. He's bleeding all over the place.'

Fenton's irritability at being startled like that made him answer curtly. 'Go and tie off the bleeding and I'll be along in a few minutes. Did Aldridge get the message sent?'

'Part of it,' answered Carnegie. 'He signalled that the house was surrounded before they put him out of commission.'

'All right. Now go and tie off Aldridge's arm and wait for me.'

Carnegie leaned forward to look out of the window. 'Is he still out there? Doctor, we're all going to get killed if we keep this–'

'Damn you, Carnegie,' hissed Dr Fenton, at last letting loose. 'Go and look after Aldridge!'

Carnegie departed, but when Dr Fenton turned again to look over at the light lorry, it was exactly as before; nothing moved at all anywhere around it. He blew out a ragged breath, wiped his forehead unconsciously, then leaned upon the wall a moment to allow his nerves to recover.

That was when he saw the shadow back in the pomegranate bush again, identifiable by the white socks. *Bert had made it!* In a second his nerves were as taut as before. He closed and latched the front window, set the curtain back in place and hastened to the pantry, where he opened that more accessible window again and waited with shallow breath until he heard the soft *shush* of elephant-ear brushing against cloth.

Bert eased up outside the window, handed Fenton his pistol in order to have both hands free to vault upwards, and moments later was back in the pantry breathing hard and looking rumpled, but showing strong teeth in a broad smile.

'Got it done,' he said. 'Caught that guy as he tried to leave the van when someone busted a bottle or a window around the far corner of the house. Caught him right under the ear with this poor excuse for a pistol.' They returned to the sitting-room. Bert handed Carnegie the pistol he had borrowed and smiled until he saw Aldridge, pale as a sheet with a broken, bloody arm dangling between his knees as Irene and the younger repair man worked over it. Aldridge raised eyes dark with pain.

'Do any good?' he asked.

Bert nodded and started fishing for his cigarettes. 'Borrowed a Colt .45 government issue from some guy who was inside the van. Telephoned our exchange operator on the emergency set and told him we were all being held hostage up here by a mob of lunatics who were armed. Told him to contact the Highway Patrol, Constable Elah, and the C.S.A. and the F.B.I. down in 'Frisco.' Bert inhaled a big lungful of smoke and slowly let it out. 'The operator thought I was drunk. But he agreed to get us some help up here. How's the arm?'

Dr Fenton, already kneeling between Irene and Frank, answered for Aldridge, whose jaw was hard-set. 'Broken below the elbow. I'll take him to the clinic.' As he rose he looked at the unconscious assassin on the sofa, started to say something, checked himself and jerked his head at Joseph Aldridge. 'Come along. At least your injury will not keep you in bed.'

Aldridge stood up a little sluggishly, but when Carnegie moved in to lend a hand Aldridge shoved him away. 'Doctor, that pellet gun you said was on the back porch – well – I think our friends out there have it now. Or one just like it. I heard the pop expelled gas makes when someone shoots one of those damned things just before the slug clipped me.'

William Carnegie looked anxious. 'If they got in here to get that gun, what's to stop them from coming back, and this time kill us all?'

Bert held aloft the ugly big GI .45 automatic. 'This, for one thing,' he told Carnegie. 'And that pistol you've got, mister ... unless your knees turn to water.'

Fenton took Aldridge towards the dining-room. As an afterthought he said, 'Mrs Potter, would you come along too? I may need a nurse.'

That wasn't true. Dr Fenton never employed a nurse. He just did not want Irene Potter out of his sight. Up until now they had all been fairly passive prisoners inside his cottage. But after the Aldridge escapade, those assassins outside might not want to be quite so agreeable. And if they happened to find that man Bert had struck down near the van, they most certainly would not feel friendly.

To reach the examination-room one had to go through Mrs Smith's spotless kitchen. Just as a matter of curiosity, Dr Fenton stepped out upon the back porch. His pellet-gun was leaning right where he usually kept it, between skirmishes with damaging woodpeckers. Carnegie had been wrong. If those men out there had a pellet-gun, or more than one pellet-gun, they had undoubtedly brought them with them.

He opened the examination-room doorway, felt along the wall for the light-switch, flicked it and moved at once to close the venetian blinds at the small window in the opposite wall. Then he pointed towards the stainless-steel table. 'Up there, Mr Aldridge. Off with the coat first, if you please.' He was very professional again. It was good being able to be that way once more.

CHAPTER SIXTEEN

HOSTAGES!

It took almost an hour to set Aldridge's broken arm even though the injury was not serious, nor the break particularly complicated. The fact was, as Dr Fenton confided, he was bushed. It was one o'clock in the morning, he had not rested very well the night before, and he had been busy most of the day, and functioning on pure nerve so far throughout the night. And he was not so young he could abuse himself this way and not be penalized. After he had sedated Aldridge he did something he never did; he stoked his pipe and smoked it as he worked. When Irene looked disapproving Dr Fenton shrugged.

'For all I know smoke may be beneficial.' He cocked a cynical eye at Aldridge. 'Feel anything?' Aldridge shook his head. He was lying back with both eyes closed.

'Just exhausted, that's all,' he muttered. 'I don't mind the broken wing, but I'd feel a lot better if I knew I'd done some good.'

'If those people outside did not think you had, I doubt if they would have reacted so violently.'

'And now,' said Aldridge, 'we've bought in, Doctor.'

Fenton puffed and worked, ignoring Irene who was standing across the table watching him. 'Mr Aldridge,' he retorted, 'we'd have bought in anyway, sooner or later. These summer nights can be awfully monotonous when you just have to sit and think.'

'I hope that repair man made his story

good,' said Aldridge, still with his eyes closed. 'But it probably sounded pretty damned preposterous to some telephone operator eating a sandwich at the night-switchboard.'

'If someone called me at one o'clock in the morning with such a story I'd think he had hallucinations too. Unless I knew him as well as Bert's people probably know him.'

Aldridge opened his eyes, spied Irene looking at him, and smiled. 'Pretty soon now you'll hear the bugle as the cavalry arrives, Mrs Potter.'

She smiled back. 'You've all been wonderful tonight, Mr Aldridge. I'll never forget any of you.'

Dr Fenton straightened up to examine his handiwork, removed the pipe and rather absently said, 'Well, if I had to do it over again, I'd swap that young repair man and William Carnegie for another pair of Aldridge's.' He clamped his teeth back upon the pipe again and reached to help Aldridge sit up. 'Your suit is ruined, of course. The coat is torn and those bloodstains will not come out of the trousers. I'd most certainly list those things on the expense account.'

Aldridge smiled. 'And overtime, like the telephone men have said. I'll expect time-

and-a-half pay for over-overtime.' Aldridge got carefully down off the table, allowed Dr Fenton to adjust a black cloth sling for his arm, and said he felt fine. Of course he didn't; even without the broken arm to throb and hurt, he couldn't have felt fine.

Irene Potter put the ruined coat around Aldridge's shoulders, crossed to open the examination-room door, and led the way back through the kitchen and the dining-room. Not until she halted in the archway dividing the sitting- and dining-rooms did Dr Fenton have any inkling of trouble.

Carnegie, Frank, and a total stranger were sharing chairs. The unconscious assassin was still lying inertly upon the largest sofa in the room, and over by the front door, which was closed, stood two rather nondescript-looking dark young men, each armed, one with an automatic pistol, the other with what looked like some special kind of sawed-off pellet-firing, soundless weapon.

The man in the chair nearest the sofa looked up. He was older, but none of the strangers appeared to be over thirty years of age. The seated man looked at Aldridge's arm, at Dr Fenton's open jacket with the butt of the Luger showing, and raised a beckoning hand without rising.

'Come right on in,' he said, using accentless English. 'Doctor, the Luger, please drop it.'

Fenton looked at the two men over by his front door. They were ready to shoot him. He lifted out the Luger and put it gently on an end-table. Then he took Irene's arm and sauntered on into the room. The seated man finally rose. He was shorter than either Fenton or Aldridge but his stockiness made him equal to Fenton in weight, and somewhat heavier than Aldridge, who was rangy rather than heavy.

Dr Fenton said, 'How did you get in here?'

The unsmiling black-eyed leader of the assassins said, 'Very easily, as a matter of fact, Doctor. We could have come in any time. There is an unlocked window in one of the rear bedrooms. In fact, we saw you and this man here, and Mrs Porter, climb out that same window only this afternoon.' The burly man pointed to the chair he had vacated. 'Sit down, Mrs Porter.' Irene obeyed. The burly man then pointed to another empty chair. 'Doctor.'

Fenton did not budge. 'I don't feel like sitting down. Furthermore, if you people harm anyone in this room you'll–'

'No threats,' snapped the spokesman for

the intruders. Then, with a softer voice, he said, 'You have nothing to threaten us with, have you?'

Aldridge moved to the chair Dr Fenton had declined and sat down. His face showed that he was suffering, finally. Evidently that sedation Fenton had given him did not last long.

The two men at the door leaned upon the wall, which was what they had been doing prior to the entrance of Fenton, Irene Potter and Aldridge into the room. One of them said, 'The man with the broken arm has a gun.'

Their leader shrugged. 'Get it then,' he ordered. 'But he couldn't do much with it with his gun-arm in a sling, could he?'

Dr Fenton felt for his pipe. He had no desire to stoke it nor light it, but at least it gave him something to do while he groped his way to an acceptance of this fresh development. The burly man watched impassively. When the pipe was lighted the leader of the intruders said, 'That is my brother on the sofa, Doctor. I appreciate what you've done for him. But he doesn't look very good to me.'

Fenton gazed at the grey, sweaty face of the wounded man, puffed a moment and did not reply until he had removed the pipe. 'You wouldn't look very good either if you'd had a bullet go through you like that. But he'll make it. The danger is haemorrhage. If he doesn't do something to start fresh bleeding, and if he gets a transfusion and proper hospitalization soon, he'll be as good as new within three or four months.' Fenton studied the burly man, beginning to accept the presence of these people in his cottage. 'I'm sure you wouldn't be interested in any advice, but if I were in your shoes, I'd get away from here as fast as I could.'

The burly man nodded. 'Perhaps. But you see, we only have to wait another little while. Porter is on his way.'

'You're sure?'

The burly man inclined his head. 'Positive. These aren't the only people we have hereabouts, Doctor.'

William Carnegie spoke up, for the first time. 'Would you by any chance consider some kind of financial arrangement to leave right now?'

The burly man turned and studied Carnegie a moment, then raised his dark eyes to the two men over by the door as though conveying to them some ironic message. One of those younger men said, 'True to type. Anything for money,' and called William Carnegie a harsh name. The burly man said nothing. In fact, he only gave Carnegie a casual look of scorn before returning his attention to Fenton, who now seemed to be spokesman for the people who had been inside the house, since Aldridge was out of things, and the two repair men were sitting there, one of them shoeless, doing nothing to attract attention.

'There is something else,' the burly man told Doctor Fenton. 'Someone got to the truck out in front while your friend there with the injured arm was trying to signal from the side window. They will bring him along in a moment for you to look at, Doctor.' The burly man turned and gazed at the older repair man's tell-tale stockinged feet. 'It was you, wasn't it?'

Bert shrugged.

'You know,' said the burly man quietly, almost pleasantly, 'for some reason you non-combatants are going out of your way to provoke us, and it doesn't make any sense. I've told Dr Fenton we mean you no harm at all. Well, I have two wounded men, both attacked by you people. Frankly, my men want retaliation.' The burly man shrugged easily the way a leader who was confident of his authority would do, and glanced at his wristwatch.

There was a light scratching at the door. Two more armed men entered the cottage. Between them they were supporting a third man who had a blood-soggy shirt and an ashen face. There was a jagged, swollen gash behind this injured man's ear. With angry faces his friends brought him to a chair, lowered him into it, then turned threateningly bleak, ugly looks upon the hostages. The burly man gave a guttural order. Those two angry young men obeyed it, but with just a hint of hesitancy. Dr Fenton noticed, and began to wonder if the burly man really did have things under control.

The wound looked worse than it was. Fenton said he'd take the injured assassin to his clinic to care for him, but the burly man shook his head. He turned to the men at the front door. 'One of you go and find a clean shirt and a jacket.' This order was obeyed instantly. The leader of the assassins then looked at Bert. 'You – since you are responsible – you go and get a large pan of hot water for the doctor, and some clean towels and soap. And in case you are tempted by the back door of the kitchen – the minute you open it you will be shot. Now go!'

Bert rose and soundlessly walked towards the dining-room. Everyone watched him depart and Dr Fenton prayed silently that Bert would not test these assassins. The burly man stepped over for a closer look at the injured man's head. He passed a judgement that Fenton thought was probably based upon experience. It also happened to be accurate.

'It isn't fatal at all, but he's going to be useless to me for a week or two. Doctor, he needs morphine to deaden the pain.'

Fenton nodded, annoyed by this layman's diagnosis but in agreement with it. The burly man reached into a pocket, held out a syringe and an ampoule. His black eyes were ironic. 'We are prepared, Doctor. Give him the injection.'

By the time Bert returned to put a large saucepan of hot tap-water upon a table and hand Fenton some clean towels, the injured man was looking less agonized as a result of the injection, but he was still sluggish and grimly silent.

'Sit down,' the burly man said to Bert, and followed the repair man with his eyes as Bert returned to his place. 'Who did you call from inside the truck? If you lie I'll kill you where you sit.'

Bert gave the burly man look for look. In a calm voice he asked for a cigarette. The burly man stood like stone for a moment, then reached into a pocket and brought out a packet which he tossed over. Bert lit up, exhaled and raised his eyes to the burly man's face again. 'I called the night operator down at Concord.'

'And?'

'Told him Dr Fenton's place was surrounded by some strangers with guns.' Bert took down a lungful of smoke. 'He thought I was drunk.'

The burly man continued to regard Bert stonily. 'How did you convince him otherwise?'

'I'm not very sure that I did. The story sounded kind of crazy to me even as I was trying to get it across to him.'

'I see. And what will he do?'

Bert dropped ash in a tray as he answered. 'Probably rout out the supervisor and report it to him. If the supervisor thinks I was drunk he'll probably drive up here himself.' Bert was a good liar. He did not waver under the burly man's stare. 'If the supervisor decides I might really be in some kind of bad trouble up here he may call the town constable in Concord and have him come up here. I don't know which he might do.'

The burly man seemed to mull this over. Dr Fenton, surreptitiously watching, hoped fervently the burly assassin would accept what Bert had told him, would possibly consider the arrival of the mythical supervisor, or a solitary town constable, no threat, and thus make an encouraging mistake.

The trouble with trying to guess the burly man's thoughts was hampered by the man's lack of expression. He neither smiled nor scowled nor seemed to hesitate. He clearly was experienced at his work, which might mean he had guessed Bert had lied.

Fenton finished washing the wounded man's head and helped the man get out of his claret-coloured wet shirt. The replacement the assassin had brought from the back of the cottage had come from Dr Fenton's own chifferobe; he recognized the shirt as he helped the injured man to put it on. It fitted like a sack but no one seemed to notice that.

CHAPTER SEVENTEEN

VARYING THOUGHTS

Irene was sent to the kitchen with one of the armed men to brew a fresh pot of coffee, but later, when the intruders tasted it, they said it was the worst coffee they had ever drunk. Aldridge and William Carnegie had two cups each and the man with the bandaged head also had two cups. His dark eyes were watery and bloodshot. He was obviously in considerable pain, but he remained silent and kept his face lowered as though he had no interest in the others or in what was going on around him.

The more seriously injured man gradually came out of his morphine-inspired stupor. Irene got him a glass of water and held his head while he drank part of it and spilled the rest of it. He looked at her, following her with his eyes when she moved near Dr Fenton again, where she always seemed to gravitate as though he were her protector.

The burly man dragged a light chair over

beside the sofa and said something in a soft, low voice to the man lying there. It was clear that the wounded man recognized the burly man but he simply looked at him, making no attempt to speak at first.

Dr Fenton washed his hands in the pinkish water of the saucepan, dried them and looked at Carnegie, the two repair men and Joseph Aldridge. There was nothing to be said or done, at least for now. Fenton took a chair between Irene and Aldridge and relaxed all over. He was dog-tired. He was also demoralized and troubled. It had occurred to him during the bandaging of the injured man's head that, prior to the invasion of his cottage by those assassins, he and the others probably had been in no direct peril, but that now, with at least six people able to identify the intruders, this comfortable situation had been voided.

He had no illusion at all about that burly man. He acted calmly and spoke the same way, but he had made it quite plain a couple of times – once when he'd sent Bert after the water and towels – that killing people would not upset him very much if at all. Probably, if he could have accomplished his duty without getting involved with outsiders, it would have pleased him, but as he had said, the people in the house had shown too much hostility; he'd been obliged to move against them, and that of course altered the status of the non-combatants.

Dr Fenton looked at Carnegie. The lawyer was sitting over there loose and slumped and grey in the face. Aldridge, too, looked to be pretty well out of things. The younger repair man, the one called Frank, had never been very co-operative nor helpful, and of course Irene Potter, regardless of how much spirit and courage she might have, was not a man. That left Dr Fenton and Bert, the older telephone repair man.

It was one of those situations where, regardless of how many people were involved, only one or two were active. Dr Fenton thought that usually was the case. He studied those two young men over by the door. Neither looked weighted by intellect but they appeared wideawake, ready to use their weapons at a moment's notice. The other two younger men in the room were injured, one with a throbbing head, the other over on the sofa. Then, of course, there was the leader of these people. Undoubtedly he could give an excellent account of himself if violence erupted. The odds, actually, were not overwhelming, except for the weapons in the hands of the intruders. That was the decisive element as far as Dr Fenton was concerned. He had no intention of risking his own life or the lives of the people with him, against guns.

A man appeared at the door, whispered to the pair of armed youths over there, then faded back as the door was closed. One of the youths went to whisper in the burly man's ear.

Dr Fenton glanced at Irene. She had also watched this small drama. Fenton knew what she was thinking because an identical suspicion had come to him: someone, probably Irene's husband, was coming, had perhaps been sighted.

The leader turned away from the man on the sofa and strolled over to stand between Dr Fenton and Irene Potter. 'It complicates things, having two injured men on my hands.'

Irene said, 'No reason why it should. You could make a very comfortable pallet of blankets and cushions in the back of the van out there.'

The leader looked condescendingly at her. 'I could,' he conceded. 'But what I meant was that in a swift withdrawal the wounded slow one down.'

Dr Fenton was lighting a pipe when he said, 'If you move your brother, you may be responsible for causing internal bleeding that could kill him.'

'Exactly,' agreed the burly man. 'But if I leave him, Doctor, your kindness will see that he heals in due time, so he can be drained dry of all that he knows about me, and about the organization.'

Fenton looked up. He was beginning to have an unpleasant hunch. 'So what do you propose doing?'

The burly man's black eyes were unfathomable as he returned Fenton's stare. 'It's a problem,' he confessed. 'I didn't want him on this assignment.' The thick shoulders rose slightly and fell. 'He's young and zealous, and now look at him.'

'I have a feeling,' murmured Fenton, 'that if he weren't your brother you'd have no difficulty in making up your mind.'

The burly man neither answered nor looked at Fenton again. His gaze was fixed upon the painfully-breathing casualty over on the sofa. Finally, without looking round, he told Irene to take his brother some water. She rose at once to obey, almost as though she had been about to do that anyway. The burly man said something in that guttural foreign language to the youths over at the door and one of them went outside, was gone only moments, then returned and made some kind of report in the same gibberish language. Finally, the burly man left his position between Irene's chair and where Dr Fenton sat, strolled to a window and parted the curtains barely enough to be able to scan the night beyond.

Fenton looked at his watch, and marvelled that so little time had actually passed since he'd returned from the clinic to find the strangers inside the house. Events that had seemed to take so much time had really only consumed moments. At any other time Eric Fenton might have thought about this. Right now he had a premonition that the waiting was nearing its end. He could tell by the way Irene and Aldridge, William Carnegie and the pair of motionless telephone repair men were acting, that the identical feeling had reached them too.

The burly man went over to confer with his armed men near the front door. They spoke so softly it would have been impossible to distinguish their words even if they had been in English, but as they weren't Fenton didn't even make an effort. He waited patiently for the older repair man to look his way, then he raised his eyebrows as though to ask Bert in silence if he had any ideas. Bert simply shook his head from side to side, very slightly and very slowly. He had no ideas; the look on his face seemed to indicate that even if he'd had any, he wouldn't have felt like implementing them with two guns behind him over by the door.

Irene returned from tending to the wounded man on the sofa. She offered a glass of water to the man with the bandaged head. He looked sullenly at her and looked away. She resumed her seat beside Dr Fenton. There were bluish shadows beneath her eyes and the long night of strain was telling on her in other ways. What she probably needed was a stiff highball, but Dr Fenton had no intention of mentioning that there was liquor in the room. They were all under a great strain, even the calm-acting burly man. Liquor would tend to negate some of everyone's inhibitions and there could be no way of predicting how so many people might react if even a little of their control was relaxed.

He was almost certain the burly man had been thinking in terms of assassinating his own brother only moments ago. A man who might feel he had to do something like this would certainly not hesitate to kill others. Especially if he had whisky in him.

Of course, it was possible he would order them all to be killed anyway, but in Eric Fenton's view the only thing they had left was time, delay, this period of waiting. He would do nothing to jeopardize it.

The burly man sent one of the armed men outside. He then returned to a front window and stood for a while peering out as though watching this man's progress. Then he did something he had not done before, he fished inside his loose-fitting olive-green jacket, brought out a packet of cigarettes and lit one. The aroma reached Dr Fenton almost at once. It had a peculiar scent, unlike American cigarettes, more aromatic, quite different. Fenton was occupied for a few moments trying to guess what kind of cigarette the man was smoking. Bert, too, seemed interested. As far as Dr Fenton had observed, these two were the only people in the room who smoked cigarettes. Bert may have been wondering whether he ought to ask the burly man for one of those cigarettes, although he had the packet of American cigarettes the burly man has tossed to him on an end-table next to where he and Frank were sitting.

Fenton was wrong. Bert spoke up when the burly man turned from the window to look round at his seated and silent prisoners. 'Smells like one of those Balkan cigarettes,' he said. It was a harmless comment; in fact under the circumstances it seemed almost frivolous.

The burly man shook his head. 'Abdullahs,' he replied. 'They aren't common here, but you can get them in any of the larger cities.' The black eyes studied Bert. 'Where have you smelled Balkan cigarettes?'

'When I was in the army we'd get leave now and then and go from Germany to France or England, or sometimes one of the border towns along the Balkan-German frontier. The people who couldn't get anything else smoked these things.'

'And you didn't like them?'

Bert shrugged. 'The smell always brought a lot of squawks when some guy came into the barracks smoking one.'

The burly man thought about this. To Dr Fenton, whose nerves were edgy anyway, it seemed that even something as trivial as this innocuous exchange might upset their fragile balance of toleration and set the burly man off. But he kept still, watching the leader of their captors.

'It's a complicated world,' said the burly man, finally, his tone as calm and controlled as always. 'If that were not so my men and I would not be here now, would we?'

Bert seemed to sense where this kind of a discussion might lead and shrugged. It was Aldridge, sitting slightly apart and looking a thorough mess, who answered. 'The trick is to get along,' he said. 'The simple thing is not to get along.'

'That is true,' agreed their captor. 'So maybe you can tell me why Americans always have to stick their long noses into the affairs of other people.'

'Peace,' replied Aldridge. 'A thousand years of doing things the old way hasn't been very successful, has it? So someone, Americans or someone, has to take the initiative and try something different.'

'Even if other people don't want things to be any different?' asked the burly man, his black eyes hard on Joseph Aldridge.

William Carnegie, silent and apprehensive for so long, spoke up. 'That's the crux. When you crowd several billion human beings together what one group does reverberates all down the line. If someone can prevent serious trouble even though he is hated for interfering, he's morally bound to try it. The alternative is frightening. It didn't used to be, but it certainly is now.'

The burly man inclined his head very gently. 'All right. That may be right. But other people happen to believe no one has the right to impose peace upon them by force. Neither do they happen to believe great powers have the right to carve up their nations to create another nation. Israel for instance.'

Carnegie surprised Dr Fenton by rushing recklessly ahead in this dispute. 'Look, I'll not deny that you have cause. Maybe even a lot of right is on your side. What I'm contending is that if we can prevent a real explosion for a while longer it will at least give all of us a little more time. And we need that very much.'

'Time for what? To ring the Arab world with arms and nuclear warheads?' The burly man's black eyes were shining, his emotions, under tight control up to now, showed through. 'You see, that's what I meant when I said it's a complicated world. We don't dare wait, but you people become more entrenched if the waiting is prolonged. And there is no peaceful answer anyway. For several hundred years strong nations have been carving up the nations that were not strong. Now, finally, we approach the end of that kind of tyranny.' He stubbed out the cigarette that had brought all this on, turned and went over to speak to the remaining young man at the door.

Aldridge and Carnegie exchanged a glance. Bert raised his eyes to Dr Fenton and gave that little indifferent shrug of his, as though to say he hadn't asked for all that alien indoctrination and hadn't been convinced by it.

Fenton looked again at his watch, then rekindled his pipe, allowed to grow cold during the dispute, and kept his eyes upon the burly man because evidently something was happening outside now.

CHAPTER EIGHTEEN

DR FENTON'S SCHEME

A man Dr Fenton had not seen before entered the house and conferred with his leader beside the front door. This man was about his leader's age, which seemed to be quite a few years older than the other assassins, at least the ones Fenton had seen up to now.

The newcomer spoke rapidly in his native tongue, but he did not seem upset. Evidently it was a matter of individual pride among these people never to show agitation, yet Fenton got the definite impression that what those two were discussing was not anything either of them were pleased about.

The stranger turned and studied the hostages. His gaze was as unfathomable as the burly man's gaze, but when the burly man suddenly went outside, closing the door after himself, and Eric Fenton, along with the others, realized they were not answerable to the newcomer, it made a difference. Whatever they thought, individually, of the burly man, he had at least done little to frighten them. They had come almost to accept his alien presence. The newcomer was an unknown quantity. It didn't help at all when he went over to peer at the man upon the sofa, then ask which of the prisoners had shot that man.

Dr Fenton had to answer although right then he would have given an awful lot not to be under that obligation.

He said, 'I did.'

The newcomer looked steadily at Fenton,

who returned the look without flinching. Then the newcomer nodded towards the slumped figure of the other injured man.

'And this one?' he asked.

Bert had to twist around to see the newcomer. 'Me,' he muttered.

The newcomer looked towards the door. Beyond it two voices were distinguishable. Then that young man who had been sent outside some time earlier walked in and resumed his position with his companion along the front wall. Fenton tried to read something from the returned man's face or stance, and failed.

Bert spoke again, evidently feeling a need to justify wounding the man with the bandaged head. 'Look, my reason for being here was legitimate – to repair a telephone that wasn't working. That guy was in our truck where he had no business being.'

The newcomer, obviously lacking the burly man's temperament, snarled at Bert. 'Shut up! When I ask you a question, you just give a simple answer!'

They all raised their eyes to the newcomer. He was indeed a different kind of man. He levelled a finger in Eric Fenton's direction. 'You are behind this resistance. We know.'

Aldridge spoke up with spirit. 'What did you expect? How would *you* react if we had done to you what you've done to us tonight?'

The newcomer said something in a bitter voice. The armed men over by the door raised their weapons. For three or four seconds no one moved and no one spoke. Fenton couldn't make up his mind whether the newcomer would actually order those armed men to start firing or not. It didn't seem likely, but then none of this affair had seemed likely right from the start.

It was a harrowing moment, but like all bad moments the longer it was allowed to run on the harder it was for the hostages to concentrate on simply being frightened. Finally, when it was beginning to seem a bit ludicrous, a bit over-dramatic, the newcomer told his men to lower their weapons. Then he smiled bleakly, hooked both thumbs in his belt and went to a front window. Fenton and Aldridge exchanged a swift look. Aldridge gave a faint, contemptuous smile as though to imply that their new jailer was a petty demagogue, a fraud of a tyrant.

The burly man came back. He and his companions went into an immediate huddle and to Dr Fenton it seemed as though something was radically wrong outside. He started to speculate about that.

Obviously, Basil Potter – or Bertram Porter as the intruders knew him – had indeed arrived. It was highly probable that he had neither come alone, nor had arrived like a sheep arriving at the slaughter. The burly man eventually left his companions and walked over in front of Irene Potter.

'I think you may be able to help us,' he said, sounding as calm and assured as ever, although Fenton did not believe he felt that way at all, now. 'We are having a little trouble outside, Mrs Porter. We have lost three men.'

Irene was pale and looked bone-tired. She did not make a sound although she obviously was listening carefully. It was Dr Fenton who spoke. 'We didn't hear any gunshots, if that's what you meant by saying you'd lost three men.'

'There were no gunshots, Doctor. Our men just disappeared. They were farther out, acting as sentinels to let us know the moment anyone came close.'

Fenton thought a moment. 'I see. You mean they have been taken prisoner, something like that?'

The burly man nodded. 'Possibly. And that means your stocking-footed friend over there convinced someone he wasn't drunk, doesn't it?'

Every warning signal in Fenton's head went off at the same time. 'Not necessarily,' he answered. 'It could more probably mean you have underestimated Mr Porter.'

The burly man slowly shook his head. 'I don't think so. You see, we have had Porter and those C.S.A. men under surveillance since they started back here from Cleveland. Our surveillance team has kept us informed. Porter only had three C.S.A. men shadowing him. That's why we've been waiting here so confidently. There are more than enough of us to overcome Porter's escort. But now there is something more threatening out there.'

'Like what?' Aldridge asked.

The burly man returned his attention to Irene Potter. 'Like a large number of men. My men have probed and are convinced that somehow we have been contained. We have you people surrounded, and it's beginning to appear as though we also are surrounded. If Porter didn't do it – and we don't think he did – that leaves only the man who used the communication system out in the truck.'

'Or my semaphore signalling with the flashlight,' stated Aldridge.

Fenton was groping in desperation for some way to stop what he thought was coming: An assassination. Perhaps two or more killings. But his mind was tired and failing. The burly man stood there looking speculatively at Irene. Finally, Fenton had an inspiration.

'If what you say is true,' he told the burly man, 'it doesn't look very good for you.'

'Or you,' murmured the leader of the captors.

Fenton nodded. 'Or us. But your concern is probably more devoted to yourself and your men.'

'And of course you have an idea that will save us, Doctor.'

'Maybe not, but if you kill us and are killed in turn no one is going to benefit, are they?'

The burly man's sarcasm continued. 'So you believe, quite heroically and incorrectly, that you and maybe one other can drive us out of here in that truck, in exchange for me agreeing to leave the others behind. Well, Doctor, let me explain a fact of life to you; if Porter and those other people out there have us surrounded, take my word for it, they will also have all the roads blocked, and, hostages or no hostages, they will get us.'

Fenton sighed. 'That's not what I had in mind. If you'll just listen for a moment, damn it, I'll explain.'

That short-tempered older man over by the door snarled at Fenton's tone and profanity, but the burly man held up a hand for silence. 'I'm listening,' he told Fenton.

'If the roads are closed to you, then obviously the ports and airfields also will be. But since it seems to be in vogue these days not to endanger hostages, I would suggest the only way you're ever going to get out of the country alive. Commandeer an aeroplane, using your hostages as assurance that it will not be shot down nor otherwise molested once its aloft, to get back to the Middle East. Become hijackers.' Fenton tried a tired smile. 'It's a very popular and inexpensive way to reach places like Cuba, Rome, even Cairo. As a matter of fact, Mister Whatever-your-name-is, there does not appear to me to be any other way. Cars are vulnerable, hostages in cars touring American highways are going to eventually be stopped. I think if you try the friendly skies of United, you will make it, even with your wounded.'

For a long moment the intruders stared at Dr Fenton. Then the burly man said, 'There is merit in the suggestion, Doctor. The problem would be to reach an airfield, wouldn't it?'

Fenton said, 'Not really. There are several within easy driving distance. The cars outside have enough fuel to reach any one of them. After that, the real problem will be to leave the protection of the cars and reach the protection of the aircraft. But with hostages, that shouldn't be impossible. Afterwards, once you were aloft, you would be safer than you've ever been before.'

The burly man turned a sceptical gaze to his companions over near the door, who had been listening closely. They lifted their eyes from Fenton to him, but said nothing. It seemed to Dr Fenton as though he had planted a thin hope in those men over there. They did not look at all elated, but neither did they scoff at his idea.

The burly man faced Fenton again. 'There is another obstacle, Doctor. Our mission is to find Bertram Porter. We cannot simply fly home having failed, even if we bring his wife with us, and you, and the others. Can you come up with an answer to that?'

Fenton leaned to ream his pipe bowl. His tiredness had miraculously vanished, enabling his mind to work swiftly again. As he settled back he saw all those faces turned towards him. What had started out as a sort of probing, delaying action, had now become something in deadly earnest. Even Aldridge and Carnegie and the two repair men were waiting for him to answer.

He said, 'Suppose I can induce Porter to go back with you?'

The burly man's brows climbed upwards. His black gaze was disbelievingly sardonic. 'How, Doctor?'

'I don't know.' Fenton reached for his pouch and started tamping tobacco into his pipe-bowl. 'I'm feeling my way along right now. Suppose you come with me, or send someone with me while I find Porter and explain to him that unless he will do this, his wife and the rest of us will not survive the night.' Fenton lit up, puffed and looked at the burly man. 'No tricks. I give you my word.'

From over by the door that mean-tempered older man said in plain English that he would go with Dr Fenton. It was a direct threat without a threatening word being used.

Fenton's gaze did not waver from the burly man's face. 'If this works, you have won. If it doesn't work, if Porter refuses, you're not one bit worse off than you already are. And if you can think of a better way out, more power to you. But at least my way, you don't have to kill anyone – even your brother – and you'll have brought off something that will, unfortunately, make celebrities of you and your people. Not here in America, but everywhere else, I'm afraid. And there's nothing impossible about any of it, really. It's being done every few weeks, isn't it?'

The burly man turned, said something curt, and one of the young, armed men at the door slid outside into the night. The other young man over there looked at his wrist, then smiled. Whatever that meant no one knew, but the older man standing with him spoke softly to his superior, the burly man, and Fenton thought from the tone that the older man was making some kind of appeal favourable to Fenton's plan.

It was a very unsettling time for Fenton and all the other captives in the room. Irene Potter was looking at the doctor as though he had betrayed her. Fenton could feel that and did not turn towards the girl. He had one little secret he had not mentioned, and if it failed Irene Potter would be as justified as would everyone else in the nation in condemning Dr Fenton for having helped murder a real hero, Basil Potter.

But desperation and the slow-gathering finale of this harrowing long night had forced him to do something. Anything was better than having to sit there with the others and be butchered, an occurrence he was more sure than ever was going to ensue if those surrounding agents and policemen out there pressed inward to capture or eliminate the guerrilla band of assassins.

Fenton, puffing on his pipe, watched the burly man and his second-in-command or whatever rank that mean-tempered man over by the door held, confer in low tones. He kept looking at those two so that he would not have to face the eyes of Carnegie, Aldridge, Irene Potter and the two repair men.

CHAPTER NINETEEN

A MOMENT OF CRAWLING NERVES

The matter of a life, or of several lives, hanging in the balance had a dream-like quality to people whose personal safety had never before been in jeopardy. Dr Fenton felt almost actual detachment while he waited for those two swarthy men over by his front door to decide whether or not to accept his suggestion. He was tired, of course, but he had been tired before and hadn't felt quite as calm and detached as he felt now. Also, he knew he had no reason to feel that way.

Finally, the burly man turned and beckoned. 'Come over here,' he said to Fenton. 'The rest of you stay quiet and still.'

Fenton crossed the room, still avoiding visual contact with his companions. He was conscious of being much larger than the swarthy men, but that was unimportant. He had been saying for years that if physical size meant anything, Goliath would have slain

David. The burly man frowned slightly.

'This man will accompany you, Doctor, and I should tell you that he is very anti-American.'

Fenton did not look at the mean-tempered assassin as he said, 'That's acceptable, but I think you'd better tell him we may not be successful in finding Mr Porter right off, so he ought to be patient.'

'Doctor,' said the burly man, 'there is a young man outside who will take you to where we believe the other side has its command-post.' Two black eyes looked sardonically upwards. 'You see, we too have technicians; they finally got that radio receiver in the repair truck working, Doctor. That's how we verified that we are surrounded by a large body of men. It's also how we pinpointed the area where their transmitter is. The young man will lead you over there. I hope they don't shoot you by mistake, Doctor.'

'Have they shot anyone yet?' asked Fenton.

'No. But my men don't walk around that far out, wearing white shirts and light-coloured trousers, Doctor.' The burly man reached, hauled the door open and gave the mean-tempered man a harsh order. Fenton did not have to understand the words, the tone of voice was sufficiently revealing.

Fenton had to halt in the darkness. All night thus far he had been in a lighted room. The abrupt transition to darkness temporarily blinded him. His mean-tempered companion reached and gave him a shove. Fenton's temper flared as he whirled.

'Keep your damned hands to yourself,' he snarled with such vehemence both the older man and the youth who was to guide them looked surprised. No move was made to touch him again although the mean-tempered man made a great show of pulling a revolver from under his fatigue jacket and holding it in plain sight. The man was evidently an incurable ham-actor. Fenton turned in scorn and motioned for the youth to lead off.

Instead of going down the hill towards the county road, invisible in the moonless night, the youth angled off around the southward side of the cottage heading in a loosely south-westerly direction. Fenton, who knew all his immediate countryside extremely well, in darkness or in daylight, was puzzled. Finally, he turned to the mean-tempered man. 'Are you sure this is the right direction? There is nothing over here, no roads or anything.'

The mean-tempered man did not answer, he simply showed large white teeth in a silent snarl and gestured for Dr Fenton to keep moving, using his gun to emphasize this order.

The youth slowed after a while. He had stumbled and that seemed to make him wary of the terrain. Dr Fenton could have warned him about the rocks over in this area but having been threatened once with the gun of the man at his back, he merely altered his own pace to match the slackened gait of their guide.

Where the youth finally halted he turned and wordlessly pointed. The mean-tempered guerrilla stepped forward to scowl off into the distance. Fenton could have grabbed him and the idea crossed his mind, but only momentarily. He was playing for bigger stakes than this disagreeable individual although he would have cheerily wrung the man's neck.

The mean-tempered man conferred briefly with the youth in their native tongue, then stepped up to Dr Fenton and said, 'They are probably no more than five or six hundred feet out there. Now you listen to me; this man and I are going to walk back a few yards and lie prone. We will both have you under our weapons, Doctor. You will call out for Porter. You will not take one step forward no matter what happens, because if you do we will kill you.'

'And if Porter comes over, how do I know you won't kill him on sight?'

'I would like doing that very much, Doctor, but I don't think we could afterwards escape, so I won't. Not here at any rate. Maybe in the air over the ocean. Maybe somewhere else.' The mean-tempered man waved his gun under Fenton's nose. 'Wait until I tell you, then call out... Doctor, I hope they don't think you are one of us and shoot you.'

Fenton nodded, his mouth dry. 'I'm sure you hope that,' he said, and waited as his captors withdrew, then melted low against the ground. The mean-tempered man hissed and Fenton turned, took a big breath and sang out.

'Porter? Anyone out there who can hear me? This is Dr Eric Fenton. I've been brought out here to talk to Porter. I'm unarmed. Porter? If you are over there listen, please. Your wife and four other people are hostages in my cottage. Unless you can effect some accommodation with these armed guerrillas I'm afraid she and all the rest of us are going to be put to death. Porter? I'd like to speak to you over here.'

Almost at once a strong, tough voice said, 'Doctor, if you'd really like a conference, come on over.'

Fenton's irritability prompted him to say, 'If you're being facetious this is a damned poor time for it. Of course I can't just walk over. I have armed men watching me. Porter, are you over there?'

A different voice, tough and harsh but recognizable, answered. 'I'm here, Doctor, cast and all. And the minute I step into their sights I'm a goner and you ought to know that.'

'Not quite,' averred Fenton. 'There is a way out. As for them shooting you – unquestionably that's what they came here to do earlier, but they know they are cut off on top of my hill, and they know they are surrounded, so they want to explore the possibility of getting away.'

Porter's retort was gruff. 'Not a chance, Doctor. If they touch my wife they won't even leave your house standing upright. They don't have a single thing to bargain with.'

Fenton fidgeted. This was taking too long;

he knew the patience, like the flash-point, of that mean-tempered man whose gun was trained on his back, would not tolerate much more of this.

'Listen to me, Porter, these people are not just simple burglars or peeping-toms. They *will* kill your wife. They will probably kill all of us as well. I think they are prepared to fight it out with you afterwards even though you get every one of them. Now listen to me – come over here where we can talk.'

'I told you before, Doctor, they'll shoot me on sight. Some of them have travelled more than five thousand miles to find me. The others are native-born but just as fanatical. Doctor, we've got the record of most of those men.'

From farther back in the darkness a man's angry voice cried out, making Fenton give a little start. 'Porter, the doctor is correct. We are not going to shoot you – not this time. You listen to what the doctor has to tell you. His proposition is good for us all. If you don't listen, well, then the other things must be done. So you can believe, this time you are safe, I guarantee it.'

A moment later a third voice sounded off. 'Okay. Porter is coming, and let me tell you people something. At the first shot we are going to strafe you with everything we've got, then we're going to close in and mop you up. Clear?'

Dr Fenton felt perspiration running under his clothes although in those small hours of the night it was not warm at all. He listened, heard footsteps, prayed desperately he had not made an awful mistake, and finally detected the uneven movement of a crippled man heading straight towards him. Potter arrived, one hand in a pocket, his face thinner and more uncompromising than Fenton had remembered it. He stopped squarely in front of the doctor, that lump in his jacket pocket unmistakable.

'I am supposed to go back with you in order to save my wife, is that it, Doctor?'

'Your wife, among others, yes,' replied Fenton, and with the guerrillas at his back and only Potter facing him, he made an exaggerated formation with his lips to convey the word *plan*. Porter looked, evidently did not understand, and relaxed slightly, now that nothing had happened.

'If I agree,' said Potter, 'how do any of us know the *Al Fatahs* won't massacre the lot of you anyway? Doctor, in case you hadn't heard, these men aren't guerrillas as much as they are fanatics and assassins. Their promises don't mean a damned thing.'

The mean-tempered man came forward, still holding the pistol in one hand. 'Porter,' he said, looking venomous in the gloom, 'this time our alternatives are limited. You will go back with us in an aeroplane, in exchange your wife and this man and the other people back at the house will be set free.'

Basil Porter scowled. 'What aeroplane?'

Dr Fenton didn't feel like explaining. As a matter of fact all he felt like at that moment was a stiff drink. The mean-tempered assassin explained about hijacking an aeroplane. Then, as Porter looked stormy, the assassin grinned and poked at Fenton with his weapon. 'It was his idea. Very nice to have such friends for us, eh?'

Porter looked at Fenton. 'You know,' he said conversationally, 'you always did strike me as a big stuffed-shirt, Doctor; an overgrown, pompous ninny.'

Eric Fenton took it. He looked squarely at Porter and neither flinched nor reddened. He even helped sustain Porter's idea of him by saying, 'Why should we all die because of you?' He made that silent pronunciation of the word *plan* again. Porter saw it, looked as dumb as before, then he sighed and pulled the revolver from his pocket to also let it dangle the way the mean-tempered man had been holding his weapon.

'Look,' he said, ignoring Fenton so hard he even turned his back to him as he spoke with the assassin. 'You go and get my wife and whoever else is your hostage with her, bring them out here and let them walk away, and I'll go with you. Otherwise,' Potter showed that tough, slow smile Dr Fenton remembered so well. 'Otherwise, Ahmed, forget it.'

The mean-tempered man stiffened. 'My name is not Ahmed,' he exclaimed and Basil Potter grinned a little wider.

'I don't give a damn what your name is – Ahmed. But if you think you've got the whip-hand let me give you a little information.' Potter gestured lazily. 'There are armed policemen completely around this hill. There are also twenty-five police dogs trained to go for the throat. And if that's not enough – Ahmed – there are more police arriving every few minutes. So, you can play it any way you like, but unless you bring my wife and those other people out here and release them damned quick, take my word for it, all of you are going home in pine boxes. That's a promise!'

The mean-tempered man was taut with outrage. Dr Fenton was almost ready to groan aloud over Potter's overt antagonism. Potter did not know the mean-tempered assassin as well as Fenton did.

Too much hung in the balance for Potter to talk like this. Fenton sought to intercede, to prevent a real argument from ensuing, by turning back and saying, 'Come along; we'd better go back to the cottage.'

The younger assassin had not showed himself up until now, but as Dr Fenton started back towards him, he rose, gun pointed. The older man, still furious, turned abruptly and stamped along after Dr Fenton. Behind them Basil Potter called out. 'Make it fast. I can't keep the police back indefinitely. As for any plan you people have – good luck.' Potter had emphasized that word. 'As for any *plan* you people have...' Dr Fenton understood. Potter had been signalling him that he knew what Fenton had been trying to convey. That was something. Not very much, perhaps, but something.

The mean-tempered man suddenly swore fiercely and freely in very good English. The younger man looked at him, shook his head and led the way back towards the front of the house. He looked glum or uncertain, or perhaps just plain frightened. It was difficult to say which it was, in the darkness.

CHAPTER TWENTY

THE EXCHANGE

The burly man was pleased, but he was also cautious. He said that in Fenton's absence he had located a local driving map of the countryside and knew where the airports were. He also said he had devised the correct plan. Nodding casually at the two repair men, he said, 'They will repair the communication line. Doctor, you will then telephone this airport to ascertain when the morning flight leaves for San Francisco, then we will cut the lines again and get ready to roll out of the yard.'

The others in the room were watching and listening, but keeping quiet. Only the mean-tempered man had something to say. 'Porter won't be enough. The C.S.A. could have their own plan. They could be double-crossing all of us...'

Dr Fenton looked disgustedly at the speaker. Even the burly man looked exasperated. 'How?' he demanded.

'Very easily,' came the quick, harsh answer. 'The moment we release all these people and have only Porter, the C.S.A. can move in and massacre all of us. Porter too. Then say he was killed by mistake in the darkness and the confusion. Remember, please, that intelligence communities have an obligation to silence people who know too much just the same as the underworld does. They might even let us get aboard an aeroplane – then have us shot out of the sky over the sea. No trace would ever be found.'

The burly man looked troubled but not quite convinced. Dr Fenton could see where flourishing seeds of doubt might blossom and spoil everything. He sought about for an answer, and found a reckless and desperate one.

'It could happen that way, but in this country if a woman were involved the public furore would be tremendous. The C.S.A. would not dare that kind of a double-cross if Porter's wife were with him.'

The mean-tempered man thought this over, then showed that arrogant smile of his. With a sly, sidelong look at Fenton he said,

'And you, Doctor; you are well known. Would they risk the publicity killing someone of your position might arouse?'

Fenton woodenly shook his head. 'I doubt it. Okay, you had better take the girl and me, along with Porter.'

This inevitably brought up a debatable issue. And the burly man thought of it at once. 'Porter said to bring all the hostages back to him and release them, didn't he? Well, you are the schemer, Dr Fenton. What can you come up with about that?'

It was no problem coming up with something, but it was going to make him look blacker than ever to Aldridge and Carnegie, Irene Potter and the pair of repair men. 'Very simple, I should imagine,' he explained. 'You will have men out there with automatic weapons, I presume.'

The burly man nodded.

'We all march out where Porter is waiting. You will then release the repair men, Carnegie and Joseph Aldridge, and as they are walking away and Porter is ready to believe you will keep your word, your men move in with automatic weapons to prevent Porter from leaving, or his wife from going with the others.'

'And you think that will work, Doctor?'

Fenton was annoyed. 'Well? What do you think? I'm gambling my life, am I not? Then obviously I think it will work.'

The mean-tempered man rubbed his scratchy jaw while the burly man stood gazing at Eric Fenton. When it seemed he might be having second thoughts, he was taking so long to approve or disapprove, the burly man nodded his head gently. 'Come along, Doctor, we will telephone the airport.' The mean-tempered man took this as his cue to go outside, presumably to recruit a man who would splice the wires so that the telephone would be functional. That left two armed youths over by the front door to watch the glum-faced hostages, who had heard every word the others had said and who exchanged hard glances among themselves but remained silent.

Dr Fenton had no trouble getting through to the airport once the wires had been mended, nor did he encounter any difficulty getting the information he wanted. There was a jet-liner that made the morning flight from Portland, Oregon, down the coast all the way to Los Angeles, every two hours all day long. It was called the 'shuttle-bus' by commuters and it would arrive at the Concord air-strip at seven o'clock, which was slightly less than two hours from now.

Dr Fenton rang off, gave the burly man this information, then felt through his pockets for his pipe. It wasn't there; he'd left it in an ashtray beside the chair where he'd sat most of the night.

The burly man offered one of his special cigarettes and Fenton declined. He neither liked the taste of cigarettes nor what they did to one's cardio-vascular equipment. For the first time the burly man smiled as he lit up and blew smoke.

'You are on the wrong side,' he said. 'We appreciate men with your talents, Doctor. Think about it between the time we get on that aeroplane and the time we get off it. Who knows; you may save your own life.'

Fenton looked squarely at the black-eyed alien. 'We're not out of this yet. If someone is stupid enough to fire a gun, on either side, we probably won't *any of us* get out of it.' Fenton previewed what lay ahead. 'We may encounter difficulty with Porter. If we do I'd strongly advise against allowing your people to use their guns. The only thing that's going to allow us to pull this off is bluff.'

The burly man looked sardonically amused. Evidently the idea of such a co-operative enemy pleased him. 'I can control my people, Doctor, and as for Porter – well – we came here to kill him anyway. If anything goes wrong he will die with the rest of us. But of course we want to avoid that, don't we?'

Fenton nodded. '*I* want to, certainly,' he said so dryly it made the burly man smile again.

Fenton looked at his wrist. 'One hour and a half,' he said. 'Suppose we get cracking.'

They returned to the sitting-room where the burly man gave an order to his armed men over by the door. They at once snapped erect and became watchful. He then told Irene, Carnegie, Aldridge and the two repair men to stand. 'You will walk out of here and follow Dr Fenton,' he told them. 'You will not speak nor do anything that will make us kill you. But above everything, you will not speak at all. Not even when we are making the exchange. Now walk out of here!'

Dr Fenton felt the searing looks he was getting. Irene Porter, lacking the venom of the looks he got from the men, was the worst he had to face; it showed a soft-sad kind of helpless reproach. Fenton walked out of the cottage ahead of the others, motioned for the same young man who had acted as guide before to move out ahead of him. Such was his altered status that the youth obeyed without being told what to do by the burly man, who moved along off to one side of the party, his fatigue jacket unbuttoned to show the holstered pistol inside.

Men appeared Dr Fenton had not seen before. He had only idly speculated on how many assassins there were, and for some reason he did not stop to analyse at the moment, it seemed plausible to him that a party such as the burly man led would be small, compact, capable of swift movement and clever manoeuvring. He had a commando-type unit in mind.

The silent hostages trudging along through the cold pre-dawn behind Fenton seemed little interested in either their guards or their surroundings. Carnegie did a gallant thing; when Irene shivered he gave her his coat, for which the mean-tempered man snarled at him to keep up and stop breaking the cadence.

The burly man glanced at his underling as though irritated by the authoritarianism of the other older man, but he said nothing, probably because the youth who was on ahead seemed to be peering ahead as he slackened his gait.

Dr Fenton knew exactly where they were, and if Porter had not moved, where Porter also was. What bothered him most right now was that Porter's invisible allies might have come up with some clever idea during Fenton's absence. From now on everything would depend upon chance, and Eric Fenton could be excused for not being at all pleased about that.

The youth stopped and signalled to the burly man. At once the burly man turned and passed along a curt order. At once two men, both quite young, walked forward. Each of them had a flat, rather fragile-looking foreign automatic weapon slung at the shoulder. These, the youth unlimbered and waited for the burly man to give another order. He simply beckoned them up close to him, then he said, 'Well, Doctor...?'

Fenton nodded, stepped up even with the youth who had guided them, peered ahead into the uncertain, watery night, and called softly.

'Porter?'

'Here,' came a prompt reply. 'Bring them on up, Doctor.'

The burly man nodded, so Fenton turned and beckoned the hostages up closer. He walked ahead a yard or two before he saw

Porter standing slouched, hands in pockets, watching. Only when Irene was recognizable in the deceptive gloom did Potter straighten his stance and show any expression.

The burly man, with his two automatic-weapons-men on each side, went forward as far as Dr Fenton's position, studied Potter, then said, 'Come close, please.'

Potter stood fast. 'Sure, Ahmed. As soon as the hostages are sent past me.'

The burly man turned, his black eyes like ice. 'You first,' he said to William Carnegie. 'You next,' he said to Aldridge. Then he gave a guttural order and the youths with the automatic weapons lifted their weapons and swung them towards Basil Potter. The burly man nodded. 'Now you come over here,' he commanded, and Potter didn't hesitate. Dr Fenton could have groaned, although a moment before he was praying Potter would do exactly that.

The burly man gestured for the pair of telephone repair men to pass across. Bert, still in his stockings, moved gingerly. The ground was rocky, the light too poor to see each stone.

Potter went over to his wife and she ran into his embrace. Fenton almost held his breath. This was the crucial moment. As

Potter stepped back to send his wife after the repair men, those two youths turned with their automatic weapons on both Potter and his wife. The burly man wasted no time. Farther back other guerrillas were kneeling, aiming at the released hostages who had stopped and were looking back, perhaps compelled against their better judgement to watch the conclusion of this bizarre situation.

Potter saw the guns pointed at him, saw the burly man's steady, hard black stare, saw Dr Fenton standing close also watching, and pulled his lips back in a snarl that was a death's-head grin of understanding. The mean-tempered assassin walked up, gun in hand, arrogant and confident. 'Walk back to the house,' he said, and flagged with his pistol. Dr Fenton looked over where the released captives stood like stone. He turned and moved out, avoiding the faces of Irene Potter and the man their enemies still thought was named Bertram Porter. It was over. Nothing had gone wrong, which was a minor miracle even though Potter and his allies out there in the night surely had agreed during Fenton's absence to avoid trouble.

The burly man quick-stepped until he was

at Fenton's side. Behind them, a yard or two back and surrounded by armed guerrillas, Potter and his wife trudged along. The burly man blew out a big breath, then said, 'Very good, Doctor.' He sounded friendly, as though he and Fenton were comrades, which in a sense they undoubtedly were, or had been at least, up to this point. 'You function well under strain.'

'Physicians and surgeons usually do,' muttered Fenton. 'It's the training. But we're not out of the fog yet.'

'Yes, I know. The aeroplane. Well, I have an idea your logic is good about that too.' The burly man smiled again at Fenton. 'Remember what I said at the cottage about thinking over my suggestion. And Doctor, if we didn't take you with us, what would those hostages say about you – about how you devised this entire thing? You see? Think it over.'

Eric Fenton looked around. 'I'll think it over, don't worry about that. Now there is something else that's got to be done. The man with the mild concussion, and your brother, should be sedated. Moving them in that van, even though we make pallets, is going to be uncomfortable.'

'And you would suggest…?'

They were in sight of the cottage. Also, off in the streaky east there was a bluish, pale blur along the horizon. Dawn was not far off.

'I don't want to give them more morphine. As you probably know one injection is often necessary, but two or three more shots are dangerous.'

The burly man nodded agreeably. He was listening closely and pacing beside Fenton as though they were friends on a stroll. 'What else can you do, then, Doctor?'

'Re-set their bandages, make them larger to cushion each man against jarring. At least as much as possible; and give each of them a knock-out sedative. It will make them bulky for your men to handle but–'

'Never mind that,' exclaimed the burly man. 'As soon as we reach your house I'll have the van got ready. You will do what you must with the patients.' The black eyes lifted. 'And Doctor... I don't want to kill you but I will. You understand?'

Fenton understood. He also understood that everything he had engineered up to this point had only been the preliminaries to what he had in mind. For a moment he felt very afraid, but only for a moment. After that he felt desperate because there was no other emotional route open to him. He had gone too far now to even think of turning back.

CHAPTER TWENTY-ONE

THE NEARING FINALE

Dawn was streaking the sooty east when Dr Fenton asked the burly man to detach a couple of men to help him get the injured guerrillas into his clinic where the full facilities for re-bandaging them were. The burly man obliged by detaching those two armed youths who had spent practically the whole night guarding hostages from a position by the front door.

These two young men, like most of the others Eric Fenton had seen since the exchange, looked a lot less gloomy than they had looked an hour or two earlier when it had first been brought home to the guerrillas that they were surrounded. One of these young men spoke excellent English but his companion was evidently one of the men who had been flown into the country from overseas. He spoke English but not very well, and it took him longer to comprehend when spoken to in English, as when Dr Fenton told this man to place the wounded man's feet at the far end of the stainless-steel table, while his companion placed the head and shoulders upon the opposite end. The other guerrilla had to snap at him in Arabic before he fully understood.

The wounded man was thirsty. Fenton sent one of his helpers for water. The wounded man was also feverish and light-headed, but he did not seem to be in any particular pain.

The wound, when bared, looked purple, ugly and swollen. Dr Fenton gave a strong dose of antibiotic to his patient, then waited until the man was helped to drink his water. Afterwards he moved the man so as to examine the gory wound where the bullet had gone through. One of the armed guerrillas grimaced at the sight of that raw and bruised hole. Fenton contradicted the man's reaction by saying the wound looked quite well.

The youth grimaced. 'Well? It looks like everything inside is trying to ooze out.'

'Swelling,' explained Fenton, 'is good. It

may not look it, but it shows a normal reaction. If there were more fever, more discolouration, and infection, we'd have something to worry about.' He eased the man down again and went to work. 'What he really needs, though, is plasma and a quiet hospital bed.'

'Otherwise,' said the youth who spoke good English, 'he will die?'

Fenton shook his head. 'Oh no, he won't die. But it would expedite recovery.' Fenton created a monstrous bandage. 'This should cushion any bumps he might get, moving him from here to the airport, and after that, on the aeroplane.'

The wounded man was fully conscious but his face was flushed, his eyes only rational for brief intervals. As Dr Fenton spoke the patient followed his face with brilliant dark eyes. Fenton went several times to his medicine cupboards and returned with bottles, with sulpha dusting powder, with all manner of disinfectants. He sent one of the young guerrillas out to the sitting-room to fetch his pipe. He sent the other one for more water from the kitchen. Then he worked very fast wrapping several flat, full flasks of colourless fluid into the monstrous bandage. When the two youths returned he was almost finished and his patient was staring quizzically at him.

Finally, Dr Fenton filled a syringe and reached for the wounded man's arm. It was violently jerked away. A prolonged period of rationality seemed to have come over the patient. He started to speak but Dr Fenton spoke first. 'Hold him,' he commanded. 'One of you put a hand over his mouth and press down to hold his head still. Fine. Now he gets the injection.'

It had been a close thing. If that dark, broad hand hadn't kept the patient's head down making it impossible for him to speak, Dr Fenton was sure the wounded man would have warned the others that Fenton had used his bandage to secrete those flasks of colourless liquid. As it was, the man's rational black eyes glared frantically, but he was far too weak to resist being held silent and motionless while Fenton gave him a powerful injection of knock-out serum.

Within moments the wounded man was inert, as slack and loose as he had ever been. Fenton took the man's pulse, found it faint but rhythmic, then listened to his breathing. Occasionally an overdose of depressants killed a patient, shocked their systems into a state of suspended respiration. In a hospital it was possible to determine through tests who might react this way and who would not, but Fenton had neither the means, nor the time, to make such tests. All he could do was give the injection then fervently hope for the best.

'Carry him back to the sofa,' he ordered, 'and bring in the other man.'

While the guerrillas were gone Fenton slid another flask of that colourless liquid into his inside coat pocket, then strolled out to fill his pipe in the sitting-room and supervise the removal of the man with the pain-racked head. As an afterthought he stopped at the sideboard, picked up a quart bottle of whisky and took it back into the clinic with him, following his aides who had to support the injured man between them. He set the bottle in plain sight upon a low shelf, motioned for the injured man to be put into a chair, then moved forward with scissors to remove the soggy bandage from the man's head.

The patient moaned pitifully. His friend who spoke fluent English said, 'Give him an injection to kill the pain.'

Fenton stopped working and looked long and hard at the youth. 'Would you like to take over?' he asked sharply. 'If not, be quiet.' The two assassins glared. Fenton relented just enough to explain. 'If I knock him out at this point he cannot hold his head up. It's hard enough making a decent compress without having him sliding down on to the floor.'

This man's head where Bert's blow had felled him, was covered with a jelly-like exudation from the wound and his ear was twice normal size. This wound in fact, although far less serious, looked much more so. Fenton made sure both the youths saw it. He pointed out where the blow had fallen and the direction from which it had been struck. He also explained that without making an X-ray photograph he could not prove it, but he was sure the patient had a concussion.

'Not too bad. That is, with plenty of rest and quiet, no more blows in the same place, no bumping or jolting, he'll be all right within a month or two. But it's anyone's guess whether he will have recurring headaches afterwards.'

Fenton kept up his running commentary as he worked. He was both adept and efficient. There was no waste motion. Finally, he got the bottle of whisky, opened it and showed it to the injured man, whose silence and discomfort seemed to warrant a drink. He handed over the bottle and said, 'Drink. Two big swallows.' The patient obeyed and afterwards made a horrible face. His friends smiled. Even Fenton smiled. He took back the bottle, hesitated, then steeled himself and took a swallow also. The whisky was good quality but it still went down like molten lava when taken straight.

Fenton forced a hard smile, looked at the other two men, then shrugged and handed one of them the bottle. 'A couple of swallows won't hurt you.' They both drank.

Fenton told one of the youths to finish winding the head compress while he got some medicine from a cabinet. Both the youths moved closer and one made careful wraps.

Fenton took the bottle of whisky to a cupboard, blandly took down a bottle of laudanum, poured it liberally into the whisky, replaced the medicine bottle, capped the whisky bottle, and waited a second or two for his heart to stop pounding. All the cameraderie for the past fifteen minutes had been indulged in just to permit him this one moment of being unobserved. It had worked.

He returned to supervise the last few

wraps, then taped the turban-like bandage in place and stood back to look critically at his work. The injured man's face was beginning to show colour, evidently as a result of the whisky. He even raised a hand to probe the bandage gingerly. Then he rose unaided. Eric Fenton smiled. 'Don't get too brave,' he said solicitously. 'You only think you're as good as new.' He gestured for the other men to help their companion, then he picked up the bottle of whisky, put it in a small black valise along with a syringe, some ampoules of morphine, several packets of fresh bandaging material, a few other odds and ends, and led the way from the clinic back out into the kitchen, and beheld an odd sight.

Mrs Smith, rising early to put coffee on to boil, had encountered the burly man in her kitchen, along with one of those young men with the automatic weapon slung from one shoulder. Mrs Smith was standing in a corner clutching her dressing-gown with both hands and looking paralysed. Dr Fenton said, 'It's all right, Mrs Smith. We've had overnight guests.' To the burly man he said with a little shrug that she was his housekeeper and was harmless. The burly man looked at the bandaged assassin, looked back at Mrs Smith and nodded.

'Take him out to the van,' he ordered. To Fenton he said, 'It looks like you wrapped pillows around my brother.'

The answer was simple. 'I told you he'd have to be protected against jarring. If he starts bleeding again you'll lose him. He's already dangerously near the low-survival level. As soon as we land you should see to it that he's given a transfusion.'

The burly man looked at Mrs Smith again. She seemed to be slowly recovering from the harrowing shock of encountering two beard-stubbled fierce and foreign-looking armed men in her kitchen.

Dr Fenton brought the burly man's attention back to himself by looking at his wristwatch and pursing his lips. 'There's not a whole lot of time to waste. We had better leave now.' He jerked his head towards Mrs Smith. 'She can't cause trouble.'

The burly man had evidently already arrived at this same conclusion. He led the way out of the kitchen with Fenton following him. At the door the doctor looked back, winked at Mrs Smith and continued on his way.

Outside, dawn was breaking. For the first time Dr Fenton saw that there was something like eighteen or twenty guerrillas. They had squeezed into the van and his car. Guns bristled everywhere. The burly man saw Fenton's expression and said, 'Doctor, they know what we are going to try to do. The hostages will have told them. The question now is – will they let us do it, or will they force and fight and get you and the Porters killed?'

Fenton knew only too well this was exactly what their situation was. He asked where the Porters were and was told they were in the van with the injured man. He looked at the sky, breathed the tangy dawn air, glanced at the burly man and said, 'There's only one way to find out, isn't there?'

They climbed into the van, which was crowded, managed to get the door closed and their driver, the mean-tempered assassin, backed clear and headed down off Eric Fenton's hilltop towards the gate below. As far as Fenton could see there was not a car in sight on the county road. It was almost too still and too quiet. The burly man stuck a cigarette in his mouth and neglected to light it, which was probably just as well. The smell in that crammed vehicle would not have added anything to the mood of the passengers.

After a while, when their driver veered off

at Dr Fenton's direction to the roadway which would take them directly to the airport, the burly man spat out his cigarette and relaxed a little. He had a pistol in his lap.

'I think they aren't going to interfere,' he said. From the back Basil Potter agreed in his tough-sounding voice.

'You're safe. With my wife and Dr Fenton to guarantee it, you're going to get aboard the aeroplane.'

Fenton tried to relax but his nerves would not cooperate. He closed his eyes for a moment, until the car lurched, then he opened them again. The road was absolutely empty, which normally it never would have been. He was certain Potter was right. They were to be allowed a clear run to the airport, and if, as he thought might be the case, arrangements had been made ahead, they would also be permitted to board an aeroplane too. It would be empty of commuters, of course, and the pilot probably wouldn't be very happy. He might even be a C.S.A. man. Not that this mattered at all.

On ahead they saw the landing-field. In the centre of it, standing entirely alone, was a large jet aircraft. The mean-tempered assassin laughed exultantly. 'You make good plans,' he said in a burst of magnanimity to Eric Fenton. 'Maybe we'll let you live after all.'

The burly man evidently didn't like that remark. He snarled something at the driver, then in English he said, 'Drive right up to the ramp. Deploy as soon as we stop. Wait until the wounded men are aboard, then come up backwards. They will be in those buildings with their guns on us.'

CHAPTER TWENTY-TWO

DARKNESS COMES AT MIDDAY

The burly man was correct. The C.S.A. agents, police and whatever other units of law enforcement were involved must have been over in the ticket, baggage, and administration building of the airport, because there were a large number of parked cars out in front, but not a single man was in sight anywhere, not even a baggage-handler, although the sleek, rather cigar-shaped Boeing 727 jet-liner stood ready with its crew of two pilots in plain sight, and its departure ground-crew of two other men. These four individuals made it a particular point to remain motionless and in perfect view, with their hands and arms visible and empty. They were the only people in sight when the cars bearing Dr Fenton and the others hove into sight, cruised out upon the tarmac and came to an easy halt close by the aircraft's boarding ramp.

Everyone piled out. Like professionals the armed assassins deployed, weapons at the ready, most of them facing the silent, seemingly abandoned building, others facing different directions and completing a loose kind of circle that gave protection to the burly man, his hostages, and the injured men.

The sun was just beginning to spread warmth. Overhead, a flawless pale sky promised ideal flying conditions. Dr Fenton stood silently with Basil Potter and his wife, feeling like someone moving in a leisurely way through a pointless dream; then the burly man gestured for Dr Fenton to accompany him up inside the aeroplane. Fenton had no illusions, he was not being invited along, he was being ordered to accompany the burly man as his hostage and, if necessary, as his shield.

They went up into the aircraft. It was empty except for the pilot and co-pilot, neither of whom were young men. When the burly man was satisfied he returned to where the flyers stood, stonily watching, and said, 'What orders have you been given and who was it that gave you the orders?'

The craggier-looking of the flyers, a man of perhaps fifty, lanky, steady-eyed and unafraid-looking, answered briefly. 'We have been told to fly you wherever you want to go, bearing in mind only that we will have to land and refuel if there is any very extensive over-sea flying involved. As for the orders ... they came from the government.'

The burly man stood gazing at the pilots a long time. Dr Fenton got impatient before the burly man turned in the hatchway and called for the wounded guerrillas to be brought aboard. Dr Fenton watched this being done with an interest that went much deeper than simply concern for injured people.

Both injured men were taken deeper into the passenger area and made comfortable. Next came Basil Potter and Irene. Dr Fenton saw how smoothly everything went off and was uncharitable enough not to attribute this to the discipline among his captors, but rather to the position the C.S.A. and allied forces took of allowing the guerrillas to escape.

It was entirely possible that Potter had conveyed to his friends, the C.S.A. people, that Eric Fenton had a plan. But whether the agents were content to rely upon Dr Fenton or not – and he rather thought they were not – whatever they had devised themselves did not include jeopardizing the lives of the hostages.

For Eric Fenton, watching the assassins close up and peel off two at a time to climb up into the aeroplane while still covered by their outward-facing companions, this was all simply a prelude to his own scheme, and the nearer the time came for him to usurp the initiative, the more implausible his plan seemed to him.

No one was relaxed, but as a youthful guerrilla squeezed past Dr Fenton to go deeper into the aircraft, he smiled. It was one of those young men Fenton had given the drink to back in his clinic. Perhaps, if he had known a little more about *Al Fatah* in particular and Arabs in general, he'd have felt even less hopeful for the success of his plan.

Arabs were forbidden by their faith to

drink whisky. Eric Fenton had been fortunate enough to have two young men at the clinic with him who were not devout adherents. The riddle was – and he would find out soon enough – how many of the guerrillas *were* devout and would not touch his bottle of whisky.

The aeroplane was loaded, the ground-crew went to work securing the hydraulically-operated hatch, the pilots went for'ard to their cubicle and the mean-tempered man, brandishing his weapon, refused to let the flyers close the door into their compartment. There was no argument. The pilots gave the mean-tempered man a couple of disagreeable looks, but that was all.

Dr Fenton went along to a seat as the aircraft began winding up. It was a sound that had always put his teeth on edge. Today, it also made his heart quicken its beat.

The burly man came and sat in the adjoining seat, nearest the aisle so that he could look aft down the full length of the craft and see all his men. A lighted sign admonished everyone to fasten lap-straps, the aircraft vibrated as its engines were run up close to maximum thrust with the brakes still locked. The burly man, in defiance of another little lighted sign, one prohibiting smoking, lit one of his Abdullahs and leaned to say, 'Doctor, I think from now on nearly all the danger is past. For all of us. What do you think?'

It was difficult to make oneself understood so Fenton merely nodded, forcing a mechanical smile of assent. He kept his medical valise close to his side and gazed out a porthole of the pressurized cabin. Suddenly, the binders were released and the aircraft, free at last to lunge ahead, began its lumbering run. Like all large aeroplanes it was as awkward as a goose on the ground, but in its natural element, airborne and free, it became smooth and relatively quiet.

They had barely levelled off from a steep climb when the mean-tempered man came down and broadly smiled at the burly man. 'I just told Porter to look down for the last time,' he exclaimed. 'His wife cried.'

Dr Fenton's prickly disposition made him glare. The mean-tempered man saw this and turned his smile to a cold sneer. 'What is it, Doctor, you don't approve?'

The burly man's head snapped up. 'Go and sit down,' he said, speaking harshly for the first time since Eric Fenton had known him. Evidently the mean-tempered man was no particular crony of the burly man. Fenton had got this impression once or twice earlier in the night, but now the burly man had either been annoyed once too often, or he thought it safe at last to loosen up and let his honest feelings show.

'Go and sit down and stop being a bully. What do you want to do, push someone into a fury and upset things? And put away that damned gun. Now go!'

The mean-tempered man reddened. He had been terribly humiliated before Dr Fenton, an enemy. He showed an expression that Fenton thought, had he been in the burly man's boots, he would not have liked. But the leader of those guerrillas was not disturbed at all. At least, if he was, it certainly did not show. Finally, Fenton and his seated companion were left alone, but for a long while afterwards the burly man kept balefully staring down deeper into the passenger section where the mean-tempered assassin had gone. Then he sighed, dropped his cigarette upon the carpet, ground it out underfoot and said, 'It is bad enough being given an assignment you don't expect to accomplish, but it is worse to be ordered to take along more men than you need, and a particular man whom you despise because you have no faith in him. Doctor, that one would have ruined everything if he could have. And now he is going to sit down there and think of a way to make this look as though I am a coward and have failed. He will tell it like this when we land.'

'You didn't fail,' said Fenton. 'In fact it looks to me as though you have done better than you were expected to do.'

The burly man relaxed. He looked tired, finally, as though he had been running on pure nerve too long. 'Doctor, I was simply supposed to kill one man. Do it without anyone knowing who did it. But now where am I? Up here thirty thousand feet in the air, with the news services whipping up indignation against me, against my organization and our cause; identifying all of my men, which was not supposed to happen.'

Dr Fenton looked out of the window. They were indeed high in the sky. He guessed they were heading towards the sea but could not be certain because of something that looked like fog hanging densely below and off to the far side of the aircraft. He looked back, saw the burly man's loosened, slack and weary face, fished in his medical valise for the bottle of whisky and said he'd go to see how his patients were coming along. The burly man eyed the bottle with lustreless black eyes, then nodded. He did not ask for a drink and Dr Fenton did not offer him one, but those black eyes followed the bottle as Fenton reached the aisle and started aft where most of the guerrillas were clustered near their injured companions.

It was time, win or lose, for Dr Fenton to make his move. He was bitter at himself for getting so involved, but if there had ever been a time for recrimination it was past.

The more seriously injured assassin was deeply and irretrievably unconscious, as Dr Fenton had intended him to be, and to remain. The other man, wearing his incongruous turban-like bandage, looked as though the drink of whisky Dr Fenton had revived him with so well back at the clinic, had quite worn off. He handed the man that quart bottle and told him to take two large swallows.

The other men watched. Fenton knelt to work with the unconscious man, who was lying upon an improvised pallet in the aisle, while the guerrilla with the injured head drank whisky under the interested regard of his friends.

Those flasks of colourless liquid inside the unconscious man's bandages were easily accessible; Fenton had made them that way on purpose. He removed each screw-cap, let the colourless fluid begin to saturate the bandaging, then sat back and took the whisky bottle from his other patient, looked around, shrugged and handed it around.

Only four men drank, which was a shock to Fenton. He did not understand why the others refused, and right then that technicality did not matter. What *did* matter was that more than two dozen men refused to touch a drop of whisky!

Meanwhile, the peculiar, and distinctive, odour was beginning to rise from the leaking bandages of the unconscious guerrilla. Fenton rose and went back to where the burly man sat, smoking again. He offered the whisky bottle. Those black eyes lingered upon the whisky, the burly man reached, removed the cap and took a large swallow. He made a horrible grimace, replaced the cap and frowned at the label.

'Terrible,' he said. 'Awful. It tastes like burnt almonds instead of decent whisky.' He looked up, saw the balefully sullen glare of the mean-tempered man upon him, and called out something harsh, then threw the bottle.

Eric Fenton held his breath. The intended

recipient fumbled the bottle but a nearby younger man caught it inches from the floor, laughed and handed the bottle to the older man. Again the burly man said that harsh word. Fenton thought he was ordering the mean-tempered man to drink. He did; took one fast swallow, then almost gagged on the second one before holding the bottle away from himself with a stiff arm. Another man took it.

Dr Fenton finally caught the scent of the colourless liquid, at the front of the aircraft. He fished a paper and pen from an inside pocket, wrote calmly upon it, put up the pen, folded the paper and shoved it partially into his topmost jacket pocket, block-printed words clearly visible. The burly man yawned and rubbed his eyes and began to list off to one side.

Fenton rose, strode unmolested up to the cockpit door, which was open, looked in, handed the anxious-looking co-pilot the slip of paper from his pocket, then closed the door and started back to his seat.

Looking down towards the mid-section of the aeroplane, Dr Fenton saw the mean-tempered man lying half off, half on, his seat, evidently held there by his leg-strap. The burly man had gone down sideways, unrestrained by the strap, and as Dr Fenton watched, he slid inertly to the floor in an awkward heap.

Farther back, the man with the bandaged head was sprawling with his head far back, also unconscious. There were four other men sliding to the floor, and among the assassins who had not drunk the laudanum-laced whisky, that colourless anaesthetic, powerful enough to induce a coma very quickly in the pressurized aircraft cabin, was working. Not a man remained unaffected. Even Basil Potter and his wife, in a seat by themselves, were turning drowsy.

Fenton stood there until he felt the dizziness beginning to reach him too, then he turned to go back to the cockpit. He did not quite make it. The aircraft banked sharply, slid yawingly off-course in an encircling return course, and Fenton fought his way to an empty seat before the over-powering urge to close his eyes caught him. He didn't even have time to look up and make certain the pilots were obeying the strict injunction he had printed for them: 'Don't open your door no matter what happens in the cabin. I have filled the air back there with a very powerful concentrate of anaesthetic.' The rest of his message was equally cryptic: 'Turn around and land again at Concord. None of us will be conscious in the cabin. The second you touch down call the police and a doctor. Disarm these guerrillas. Call in the Central Security Agency. My name is Eric Fenton. When I come round I'll explain what has happened.'

The aeroplane was still in a steep, banking turn heading back towards its point of origin. Eric Fenton felt that in the last fleeting moments of consciousness. He dimly knew he had won. Then he let go all over and allowed the whirling blackness to engulf him, sweeping him down and down until he knew nothing more.

The publishers hope that this book has given you enjoyable reading. Large Print Books are especially designed to be as easy to see and hold as possible. If you wish a complete list of our books please ask at your local library or write directly to:

Dales Large Print Books
Magna House, Long Preston,
Skipton, North Yorkshire.
BD23 4ND